Emma offered Roele cake. "You have been very kind and I'm so grateful."

"Of course," the doctor replied.

Emma was instantly and unreasonably disappointed that he hadn't shown more interest or concern. She said stiffly, "Miss Johnson told me that you don't live here, that you are filling in for another doctor."

"Yes, I shall be sorry to leave...."

"Not yet?"

His heavy-lidded eyes gleamed. "No, no. I'm looking forward to the summer here."

Dear Reader,

We'd like to take this opportunity to pay tribute to Betty Neels, who sadly passed away last year. Betty was one of our best-loved authors. As well as being a wonderfully warm and thoroughly charming individual, Betty led a fascinating life even before becoming a writer, and her publishing record was impressive.

Betty spent her childhood and youth in Devonshire, England, before training as a nurse and midwife. She was an army nursing sister during the war, married a Dutchman and subsequently lived in Holland for fourteen years. On retirement from nursing, Betty started to write, incited by a lady in a library bemoaning the lack of romantic novels.

Over her thirty-year writing career, Betty wrote more than 134 novels, and was published in more than one hundred international markets. She continued to write into her ninetieth year, remaining as passionate about her characters and stories then as she was in her very first book.

Betty will be greatly missed, both by her friends within Harlequin and by her legions of loyal readers around the world. Betty was a prolific writer, and we have a number of new titles to feature in our forthcoming publishing programs. Betty has left a lasting legacy through her heartwarming novels, and she will always be remembered as a truly delightful person who brought great happiness to many.

The Editors
Harlequin Romance®

EMMA'S WEDDING
Betty Neels

You are invited to a
WHITE WEDDING

HARLEQUIN®

TORONTO • NEW YORK • LONDON
AMSTERDAM • PARIS • SYDNEY • HAMBURG
STOCKHOLM • ATHENS • TOKYO • MILAN • MADRID
PRAGUE • WARSAW • BUDAPEST • AUCKLAND

ISBN 0-373-15945-5

EMMA'S WEDDING

First North American Publication 2002.

Copyright © 2001 by Betty Neels.

This edition published by arrangement with Harlequin Books S.A.

® and TM are trademarks of the publisher. Trademarks indicated with
® are registered in the United States Patent and Trademark Office, the
Canadian Trade Marks Office and in other countries.

Visit us at www.eHarlequin.com

Printed in U.S.A.

CHAPTER ONE

THERE were three people in the room: an elderly man with a fringe of white hair surrounding a bald pate and a neat little beard, a lady of uncertain years and once very pretty, her faded good looks marred by a look of unease, and, sitting at the table between them, a girl, a splendid young woman as to shape and size, with carroty hair bunched untidily on top of her head and a face which, while not beautiful or even pretty, was pleasing to look at, with wide grey eyes, a haughty nose and a wide mouth, gently curved.

The elderly man finished speaking, shuffled the papers before him and adjusted his spectacles, and when her mother didn't speak, only sat looking bewildered and helpless, the girl spoke.

'We shall need your advice, Mr Trump. This is a surprise—we had no idea...Father almost never mentioned money matters to either Mother or me, although some weeks before he died...' her voice faltered for a moment '...he told me that he was investing in some scheme which would make a great deal of money, and when I asked him about it he laughed and said it was all rather exciting and I must wait and see.'

Mr Trump said dryly, 'Your father had sufficient funds to live comfortably and leave both your mother and you provided for. He invested a considerable amount of his capital in this new computer company set up by a handful of unscrupulous young men and for a few weeks it made profits, so that your father invested the rest of his capital in it. Inevitably, the whole thing fell apart, and he and a number of the other investors lost every penny. In order to avoid bankruptcy you will need to sell this house, the car, and much of the furniture. You have some good pieces here which should sell well.'

He glanced at her mother and added, 'You do understand what I have told you, Mrs Dawson?'

'We shall be poor.' She gave a little sob. 'There won't be any money. How are we to live?' She looked around her. 'My lovely home—and how am I to go anywhere if we haven't any car? And clothes? I won't be shabby.' She began to cry in real earnest. 'Where shall we live?' And before anyone could speak she added, 'Emma, you must think of something…'

'Try not to get upset, Mother. If this house and everything else sells well enough to pay off what's owing, we can go and live at the cottage in Salcombe. I'll get a job and we shall manage very well.'

Mr Trump nodded his bald head. 'Very sensible. I'm fairly certain that once everything is sold there will be enough to pay everything off and even have a small amount over. I imagine it won't be too hard to find work during the summer season at least, and there might even be some small job which you might undertake, Mrs Dawson.'

'A job? Mr Trump, I have never worked in my life and I have no intention of doing so now.' She dissolved into tears again. 'My dear husband would turn in his grave if he could hear you suggest it.'

Mr Trump put his papers in his briefcase. Mrs Dawson he had always considered to be a charming little lady, rather spoilt by her husband but with a gentle, rather helpless manner which appealed to his old-fashioned notions of the weaker sex, but now, seeing the petulant look on her face, he wondered if he had been mistaken. Emma, of course, was an entirely different kettle of fish, being a sensible young woman, full of energy, kind and friendly—and there was some talk of her marrying. Which might solve their difficulties. He made his good-byes, assured them that he would start at once on the unravelling of their affairs, then went out to his car and drove away.

Emma went out of the rather grand drawing room and crossed the wide hall to the kitchen. It was a large house, handsomely furnished with every mod con Mrs Dawson had expressed a wish to have. There was a daily housekeeper too, and a cheerful little woman who came twice a week to do the rough work.

Emma put on the kettle, laid a tea tray, found biscuits and, since the housekeeper had gone out for her half-day, looked through the cupboards for the cake tin. She and her mother might have been dealt a bitter blow, but tea and a slice of Mrs Tims's walnut cake would still be welcome. For as long as possible, reflected Emma.

Mrs Dawson was still sitting in her chair, dabbing her wet eyes.

She watched Emma pour the tea and hand her a cup. 'How can I possibly eat and drink,' she wanted to know in a tearful voice, 'when our lives are in ruins?'

All the same she accepted a slice of cake.

Emma took a bite. 'We shall have to give Mrs Tims notice. Do you pay her weekly or monthly, Mother?'

Mrs Dawson looked vague. 'I've no idea. Your father never bothered me with that kind of thing. And that woman who comes in to clean—Ethel—what about her?'

'Shall I talk to them both and give them notice? Though they'll expect something extra as Father's death gave them no warning.'

Emma drank some tea and swallowed tears with it. She had loved her father, although they had never been close and the greater part of his paternal affection had been given to her brother James, twenty-three years old and four years her junior. And presently, most unfortunately, backpacking round the world after leaving university with a disappointing degree in science.

They weren't even quite sure where he was at the moment; his last address had been Java, with the prospect of Australia, and even if they had had an address and he'd come home at once she didn't think that he would have been of much help.

He was a dear boy, and she loved him, but her mother and father had spoilt him so that although he was too nice a young man to let it ruin his nature, it had tended to make him easygoing and in no hurry to settle down to a serious career.

He had had a small legacy from their grandmother when she died, and that had been ample to take care of his travels. She thought it unlikely that he would break off his journey, probably arguing that he was on the other side of the world and that Mr Trump would deal with his father's affairs, still under the impression that he had left his mother and sister in comfortable circumstances.

Emma didn't voice these thoughts to her mother but instead settled that lady for a nap and went back to the kitchen to prepare for their supper. Mrs Tims would have left something ready to be cooked and there was nothing much to do. Emma sat down at the table, found pencil and paper, and wrote down everything which would have to be done.

A great deal! And she couldn't hope to do it all herself. Mr Trump would deal with the complicated financial situation, but what about the actual selling of the house and their possessions? And what would they be allowed to keep of those? Mr Trump had mentioned an overdraft at the bank, and money which had been borrowed from friends with the promise that it would be returned to them with handsome profits.

Emma put her head down on the table and cried. But not for long. She wiped her eyes, blew her nose and picked up her pencil once more.

If they were allowed to keep the cottage at least they would have a rent-free home and one which she had always loved, although her mother found the little town of Salcombe lacking in the kind of social life she liked, but it would be cheaper to live there for that very reason. She would find work; during the summer months there was bound to be a job she could do—waitressing, or working in one of the big hotels or a shop. The winter might not be as easy, the little town sank into peace and quiet, but Kingsbridge was only a bus ride away, and that was a bustling small town with plenty of shops and cafés...

Feeling more cheerful, Emma made a list of their own possessions which surely they would be allowed to keep. Anything saleable they must sell, although she thought it was unlikely that her mother would be prepared to part with her jewellery, but they both had expensive clothes—her father had never grudged them money for those—and they would help to swell the kitty.

She got the supper then, thinking that it was a pity that Derek wouldn't be back in England for three more days. They weren't engaged, but for some time now their future together had become a foregone conclusion. Derek was a serious young man and had given her to understand that once he had gained the promotion in the banking firm for which he worked they would marry.

Emma liked him, indeed she would have fallen in love with him and she expected to do that without much difficulty, but although he was devoted to her she had the idea that he didn't intend to show his proper feelings until he proposed. She had been quite content; life wasn't going to be very exciting, but a kind husband who would cherish one, and any children, and give one a comfortable home should bring her happiness.

She wanted to marry, for she was twenty-seven, but ever since she had left school there had always been a reason why she couldn't leave home, train for something and be independent. She had hoped that when James had left the university she could be free, but when she had put forward her careful plans it had been to discover that he had already arranged to be away for two years at least, and her mother had become quite hysterical at the idea of not having one or other of her children at home with her. And, of course, her father had agreed...

Perhaps her mother would want her to break off with Derek, but she thought not. A son-in-law in comfortable circumstances would solve their difficulties...

During the next three days Emma longed for Derek's return. It seemed that the business of being declared bankrupt entailed a mass of paperwork, with prolonged and bewildering visits from severe-looking men with briefcases. Since her mother declared that she would have nothing to do with any of it, Emma did her best to answer their questions and fill in the forms they offered.

'But I'll not sign anything until Mr Trump has told me that I must,' she told them.

It was all rather unnerving; she would have liked a little time to grieve about her father's death, but there was no chance of that. She went about her household duties while her mother sat staring at nothing and weeping, and Mrs Tims and Ethel worked around the house, grim-faced at the unexpectedness of it all.

Derek came, grave-faced, offered Mrs Dawson quiet condolences and went with Emma to her father's study. But if she had expected a shoulder to cry on she didn't get it. He was gravely concerned for her, and kind, but she knew at once that he would never marry her now. He had an important job in the banking world, and marrying the daughter of a man who had squandered a fortune so recklessly was hardly going to enhance his future.

He listened patiently to her problems, observed that she was fortunate to have a sound man such as Mr Trump to advise her, and told her to be as helpful with 'Authority' as possible.

'I'm afraid there are no mitigating circumstances,' he told her. 'I looked into the whole affair when I got back today. Don't attempt to contest anything, whatever you do. Hopefully there will be enough money to clear your father's debts once everything is sold.'

Emma sat looking at him—a good-looking man in his thirties, rather solemn in demeanour, who had nice manners, was honest in his dealings, and not given to rashness of any sort. She supposed that it was his work which had driven the warmth from his heart and allowed common sense to replace the urge to help her at all costs and, above all, to comfort her.

'Well,' said Emma in a tight little voice, 'how fortunate it is that you didn't give me a ring, for I don't need to give it back.'

He looked faintly surprised. 'I wasn't aware that we had discussed the future,' he told her.

'There is no need, is there? I haven't got one, have I? And yours matters to you.'

He agreed gravely. 'Indeed it does. I'm glad, Emma, that you are sensible enough to realise that, and I hope that you will too always consider me as a friend. If I can help in any way… If I can help financially?'

'Mr Trump is seeing to the money, but thank you for offering. We shall be able to manage very well once everything is sorted out.'

'Good. I'll call round from time to time and see how things are…'

'We shall be busy packing up—there is no need.' She added in a polite hostess voice, 'Would you like a cup of coffee before you go?'

'No—no, thank you. I'm due at the office in the morning and I've work to do first.'

He wished Mrs Dawson goodbye, and as Emma saw him to the door he bent to kiss her cheek. 'If ever you should need help or advice…'

'Thank you, Derek,' said Emma. Perhaps she should make a pleasant little farewell speech, but if she uttered another word she would burst into tears.

'How fortunate that you have Derek,' said Mrs Dawson when Emma joined her. 'I'm sure he'll know what's best to be done. A quiet wedding as soon as possible.'

'Derek isn't going to marry me, Mother. It would interfere with his career.'

A remark which started a flood of tears from her mother.

'Emma, I can't believe it. It isn't as if he were a young man with no money or prospects. There's no reason why you shouldn't marry at once.' She added sharply, 'You didn't break it off, did you? Because if you did you're a very stupid girl.'

'No, Mother, it's what Derek wishes.' Emma felt sorry for her mother. She looked so forlorn and pretty, and so in need of someone to make life easy for her as it always had been. 'I'm sorry, but he has got his career to consider, and marrying me wouldn't help him at all.'

'I cannot think what came over your father...'

'Father did it because he wanted us to have everything we could possibly want,' said Emma steadily. 'He never grudged you anything, Mother.'

Mrs Dawson was weeping again. 'And look how he has left us now. It isn't so bad for you, you're young and can go to work, but what about me? My nerves have never allowed me to do anything strenuous and all this worrying has given me a continuous headache. I feel that I am going to be ill.'

'I'm going to make you a milky drink and put a warm bottle in your bed, Mother. Have a bath, and when you're ready I'll come up and make sure that you are comfortable.'

'I shall never be comfortable again,' moaned
Mrs Dawson.

She looked like a small woebegone child and
Emma gave her a hug; the bottom had fallen
out of her mother's world and, although life
would never be the same again, she would do
all that she could to make the future as happy
as possible.

For a moment she allowed her thoughts to
dwell on her own future. Married to Derek she
would have had a pleasant, secure life: a home
to run, children to bring up, a loving husband
and as much of a social life as she would wish.
But now that must be forgotten; she must make
a happy life for her mother, find work, make
new friends. Beyond that she didn't dare to
think. Of course James would come home eventually, but he would plan his own future, cheerfully taking it for granted that she would look
after their mother, willing to help if he could
but not prepared to let it interfere with his plans.

The house sold quickly, the best of the furniture
was sold, and the delicate china and glass. Most
of the table silver was sold too, and the house,
emptied of its contents, was bleak and unwel-
coming. But there was still a great deal to do;
even when Emma had packed the cases of un-
saleable objects—the cheap kitchen china, the

saucepans, the bed and table linen that they were allowed to keep—there were the visits from her parents' friends, come to commiserate and eager, in a friendly way, for details. Their sympathy was genuine but their offers of help were vague. Emma and her mother must come and stay as soon as they were settled in; they would drive down to Salcombe and see them. Such a pretty place, and how fortunate that they had such a charming home to go to...

Emma, ruthlessly weeding out their wardrobes, thought it unlikely that any of their offers would bear fruit.

Mr Trump had done his best, and every debt had been paid, leaving a few hundred in the bank. Her mother would receive a widow's pension, but there was nothing else. Thank heaven, reflected Emma, that it was early in April and a job, any kind of job, shouldn't be too hard to find now that the season would be starting at Salcombe.

They left on a chilly damp morning—a day winter had forgotten and left behind. Emma locked the front door, put the key through the letterbox and got into the elderly Rover they had been allowed to keep until, once at Salcombe, it was to be handed over to the receivers. Her father's Bentley had gone, with everything else.

She didn't look back, for if she had she might have cried and driving through London's traffic didn't allow for tears. Mrs Dawson cried. She cried for most of their long journey, pausing only to accuse Emma of being a hard-hearted girl with no feelings when she suggested that they might stop for coffee.

They reached Salcombe in the late afternoon and, as it always did, the sight of the beautiful estuary with the wide sweep of the sea beyond lifted Emma's spirits. They hadn't been to the cottage for some time but nothing had changed; the little house stood at the end of a row of similar houses, their front gardens opening onto a narrow path along the edge of the water, crowded with small boats and yachts, a few minutes' walk from the main street of the little town, yet isolated in its own peace and quiet.

There was nowhere to park the car, of course. Emma stopped in the narrow street close by and they walked along the path, opened the garden gate and unlocked the door. For years there had been a local woman who had kept an eye on the place. Emma had written to her and now, as they went inside, it was to find the place cleaned and dusted and groceries and milk in the small fridge.

Mrs Dawson paused on the doorstep. 'It's so small,' she said in a hopeless kind of voice, but

Emma looked around her with pleasure and relief. Here was home: a small sitting room, with the front door and windows overlooking the garden, a smaller kitchen beyond and then a minute back yard, and, up the narrow staircase, two bedrooms with a bathroom between them. The furniture was simple but comfortable, the curtains a pretty chintz and there was a small open fireplace.

She put her arm round her mother. 'We'll have a cup of tea and then I'll get the rest of the luggage and see if the pub will let me put the car in their garage until I can hand it over.'

She was tired when she went to bed that night; she had seen to the luggage and the car, lighted a small log fire and made a light supper before seeing her mother to her bed. It had been a long day, she reflected, curled up in her small bedroom, but they were here at last in the cottage, not owing a farthing to anyone and with a little money in the bank. Mr Trump had been an elderly shoulder to lean on, which was more than she could say for Derek. 'Good riddance to bad rubbish,' said Emma aloud.

All the same she had been hurt.

In the morning she went to the pub and persuaded the landlord to let her leave the car there until she could hand it over, and then went into the main street to do the shopping. Her mother had declared herself exhausted after their long drive on the previous day and Emma had left her listlessly unpacking her clothes. Not a very good start to the day, but it was a fine morning and the little town sparkled in the sunshine.

Almost all the shops were open, hopeful of early visitors, and she didn't hurry with her shopping, stopping to look in the elegant windows of the small boutiques, going to the library to enrol for the pair of them, arranging for milk to be delivered, ordering a paper too, and at the same time studying the advertisements in the shop window. There were several likely jobs on offer. She bought chops from the butcher, who remembered her from previous visits, and crossed the road to the greengrocer. He remembered her too, so that she felt quite light-hearted as she made her last purchase in the baker's.

The delicious smell of newly baked bread made her nose quiver. And there were rolls and pasties, currant buns and doughnuts. She was hesitating as to which to buy when someone else came into the shop. She turned round to look and encountered a stare from pale blue eyes so intent that she blushed, annoyed with herself for doing that just because this large man was staring. He was good-looking too, in a rugged kind of way, with a high-bridged nose and a thin mouth. He was wearing an elderly jersey and cords and his hair needed a good brush...

He stopped staring, leaned over her, took two pasties off the counter and waved them at the baker's wife. And now the thin mouth broke into a smile. 'Put it on the bill, Mrs Trott,' he said, and was gone.

Emma, about to ask who he was, sensed that Mrs Trott wasn't going to tell her and prudently held her tongue. He must live in the town for he had a bill. He didn't look like a fisherman or a farm worker and he wouldn't own a shop, not dressed like that, and besides he didn't look like any of those. He had been rude, staring like that; she had no wish to meet him again but it would be interesting to know just who he was.

She went back to the cottage and found a man waiting impatiently to collect the car and, what with one thing and another, she soon forgot the man at the baker's.

It was imperative to find work but she wasn't going to rush into the first job that was vacant. With a little wangling she thought that she could manage two part-time jobs. They would cease at the end of the summer and even one part-time job might be hard to find after that.

'I must just make hay while the sun shines,' said Emma, and over the next few days scanned the local newspapers. She went from one end of the town to the other, sizing up what was on offer. Waitresses were wanted, an improver was needed at the hairdressers—but what was an improver? Chambermaids at the various hotels, an assistant in an arts and crafts shop, someone to clean holiday cottages between lets, and an educated lady to assist the librarian at the public library on two evenings a week…

It was providential that while out shopping with her mother they were accosted by an elderly lady who greeted them with obvious pleasure.

'Mrs Dawson—and Emma, isn't it? Perhaps you don't remember me. You came to the hotel to play bridge. I live at the hotel now that my husband has died and I'm delighted to see a face I know…' She added eagerly, 'Let's go and have coffee together and a chat. Is your husband with you?'

'I am also a widow—it's Mrs Craig, isn't it? I do remember now; we had some pleasant afternoons at bridge. My husband died very recently, and Emma and I have come to live here.'

'I'm so very sorry. Of course you would want to get away from Richmond for a time. Perhaps we could meet soon and then arrange a game of bridge later?'

Mrs Dawson brightened. 'That would be delightful…'

'Then you must come and have tea with me sometimes at the hotel.' Mrs Craig added kindly, 'You need to have a few distractions, you know.' She smiled at Emma. 'I'm sure you have several young friends from earlier visits?'

Emma said cheerfully, 'Oh, yes, of course,' and added, 'I've one or two calls to make now, while you have coffee. It is so nice to meet you again, Mrs Craig.' She looked at her mother. 'I'll see you at home, Mother.'

She raced away. The rest of the shopping could wait. Here was the opportunity to go to the library...

The library was at the back of the town, and only a handful of people were wandering round the bookshelves. There were two people behind the desk: one a severe-looking lady with a no-nonsense hair style, her companion a girl with a good deal of blonde hair, fashionably tousled, and with too much make-up on her pretty face. She looked up from the pile of books she was arranging and grinned at Emma as she came to a halt and addressed the severe lady.

'Good morning,' said Emma. 'You are advertising for an assistant for two evenings a week. I should like to apply for the job.'

The severe lady eyed her. She said shortly, 'My name is Miss Johnson. Are you experienced?'

'No, Miss Johnson, but I like books. I have
A levels in English Literature, French, Modern
Art and Maths. I am twenty-seven years old and
I have lived at home since I left school. I have
come here to live with my mother and I need a
job.'

'Two sessions a week, six hours, at just under
five pounds an hour.' Miss Johnson didn't
sound encouraging. 'Five o'clock until eight on
Tuesdays and Thursdays. Occasionally extra
hours, if there is sickness or one of us is on
holiday.' She gave what might be called a la-
dylike sniff. 'You seem sensible. I don't want
some giddy girl leaving at the end of a week...'

'I should like to work here if you will have
me,' said Emma. 'You will want references...?'

'Of course, and as soon as possible. If they
are satisfactory you can come on a week's trial.'

Emma wrote down Mr Trump's address and
phone number and then Dr Jakes's who had
known her for years. 'Will you let me know or
would you prefer me to call back? We aren't
on the phone yet. It's being fitted shortly.'

'You're in rooms or a flat?'

'No, we live at Waterside Cottage, the end
one along Victoria Quay.'

Miss Johnson looked slightly less severe.
'You are staying there? Renting the cottage for
the summer?'

'No, it belongs to my mother.'

The job, Emma could see, was hers.

She bade Miss Johnson a polite goodbye and went back into the main street; she turned into a narrow lane running uphill, lined by small pretty cottages. The last cottage at the top of the hill was larger than the rest and she knocked on the door.

The woman who answered the door was still young, slim and tall and dressed a little too fashionably for Salcombe. Her hair was immaculate and so was her make-up.

She looked Emma up and down and said, 'Yes?'

'You are advertising for someone to clean holiday cottages...'

'Come in.' She led Emma into a well-furnished sitting room.

'I doubt if you'd do. It's hard work— Wednesdays and Saturdays, cleaning up the cottages and getting them ready for the next lot. And a fine mess some of them are in, I can tell you. I need someone for those two days. From ten o'clock in the morning and everything ready by four o'clock when the next lot come.'

She waved Emma to a chair. 'Beds, bathroom, loo, Hoovering. Kitchen spotless—and that means cupboards too. You come here and collect the cleaning stuff and bedlinen and hand

in the used stuff before you leave. Six hours
work a day, five pounds an hour, and tips if
anyone leaves them.'

'For two days?'

'That's what I said. I'll want references.
Local, are you? Haven't seen you around. Can't
stand the place myself. The cottages belonged
to my father and I've taken them over for a year
or two. I'm fully booked for the season.'

She crossed one elegantly shod foot over the
other. 'Week's notice on either side?'

'I live here,' said Emma, 'and I need a job.
I'd like to come if you are satisfied with my
references.'

'Please yourself, though I'd be glad to take
you on. It isn't a job that appeals to the girls
around here.'

It didn't appeal all that much to Emma, but
sixty pounds a week did...

She gave her references once more, and was
told she'd be told in two days' time. 'If I take
you on you'll need to be shown round. There's
another girl cleans the other two cottages across
the road.'

Emma went home, got the lunch and listened
to her mother's account of her morning with
Mrs Craig. 'She has asked me to go to the hotel
one afternoon for a rubber of bridge.' She hes-

itated. 'They play for money—quite small stakes...'

'Well,' said Emma, 'you're good at the game, aren't you? I dare say you won't be out of pocket. Nice to have found a friend, and I'm sure you'll make more once the season starts.'

Two days later there was a note in the post. Her references for the cleaning job were satisfactory, she could begin work on the following Saturday and in the meantime call that morning to be shown her work. It was signed Dulcie Brooke-Tigh. Emma considered that the name suited the lady very well.

She went to the library that afternoon and Miss Johnson told her unsmilingly that her references were satisfactory and she could start work on Tuesday. 'A week's notice and you will be paid each Thursday evening.'

Emma, walking on air, laid out rather more money than she should have done at the butchers, and on Sunday went to church with her mother and said her prayers with childlike gratitude.

The cleaning job was going to be hard work. Mrs Brooke-Tigh, for all her languid appearance, was a hard-headed businesswoman, intent on making money. There was enough work for two people in the cottages, but as long as she could get a girl anxious for the job she wasn't bothered. She had led Emma round the two cottages she would be responsible for, told her to start work punctually and then had gone back into her own cottage and shut the door. She didn't like living at Salcombe, but the holiday cottages were money-spinners...

The library was surprisingly full when Emma, punctual to the minute, presented herself at the desk.

Miss Johnson wasted no time on friendly chat. 'Phoebe will show you the shelves, then come back here and I will show you how to stamp the books. If I am busy take that trolley of returned books and put them back on the shelves. And do it carefully; I will not tolerate slovenly work.'

Which wasn't very encouraging, but Phoebe's cheerful wink was friendly. The work wasn't difficult or tiring, and Emma, who loved books, found the three hours had passed almost too quickly. And Miss Johnson, despite her austere goodnight, had not complained.

Emma went back to the cottage to eat a late supper and then sit down to do her sums. Her mother had her pension, of course, and that plus the money from the two jobs would suffice to keep them in tolerable comfort. There wouldn't be much over, but they had the kind of expensive, understated clothes which would last for several years... She explained it all to her mother, who told her rather impatiently to take over their finances. 'I quite realise that I must give up some of my pension, dear, but I suppose I may have enough for the hairdresser and small expenses?'

Emma did some sums in her head and offered a generous slice of the pension—more than she could spare. But her mother's happiness and peace of mind were her first concern; after years of living in comfort, and being used to having everything she wanted within reason, she could hardly be expected to adapt easily to their more frugal way of living.

On Saturday morning she went to the cottages. She had told her mother that she had two jobs, glossing over the cleaning and enlarging on the library, and, since Mrs Dawson was meeting Mrs Craig for coffee, Emma had said that she would do the shopping and that her mother wasn't to wait lunch if she wasn't home.

She had known it was going to be hard work and it was, for the previous week's tenants had made no effort to leave the cottage tidy, let alone clean. Emma cleaned and scoured, then Hoovered and made beds and tidied cupboards, cleaned the cooker and the bath, and at the end of it was rewarded by Mrs Brooke-Tigh's nod of approval and, even better than that, the tip she had found in the bedroom—a small sum, but it swelled the thirty pounds she was paid as she left.

'Wednesday at ten o'clock,' said Mrs Brooke-Tigh.

Emma walked down the lane with the girl who cleaned the other two cottages.

'Mean old bag,' said the girl. 'Doesn't even give us a cup of coffee. Think you'll stay?'

'Oh, yes,' said Emma.

The future, while not rosy, promised security just so long as people like Mrs Brooke-Tigh needed her services.

When she got home her mother told her that Mrs Craig had met a friend while they were having their coffee and they had gone to the little restaurant behind the boutique and had lunch. 'I was a guest, dear, and I must say I enjoyed myself.' She smiled. 'I seem to be making friends. You must do the same, dear.'

Emma said, 'Yes, Mother,' and wondered if she would have time to look for friends. Young women of her own age? Men? The thought crossed her mind that the only person she would like to see again was the man in the baker's shop.

CHAPTER TWO

EMMA welcomed the quiet of Sunday. It had been a busy week, with its doubts and worries and the uncertainty of coping with her jobs. But she had managed. There was money in the household purse and she would soon do even better. She went with her mother to church and was glad to see that one or two of the ladies in the congregation smiled their good mornings to her mother. If her mother could settle down and have the social life she had always enjoyed things would be a lot easier. I might even join some kind of evening classes during the winter, thought Emma, and meet people…

She spent Monday cleaning the cottage, shopping and hanging the wash in the little back yard, while her mother went to the library to choose a book. On the way back she had stopped to look at the shops and found a charming little scarf, just what she needed to cheer up her grey dress. 'It was rather more than I wanted to spend, dear,' she explained, 'but exactly what I like, and I get my pension on Thursday...'

The library was half empty when Emma got there on Tuesday evening.

'WI meeting,' said Miss Johnson. 'There will be a rush after seven o'clock.'

She nodded to a trolley loaded with books. 'Get those back onto the shelves as quickly as you can. Phoebe is looking up something for a visitor.'

Sure enough after an hour the library filled up with ladies from the WI, intent on finding something pleasant to read, and Emma, intent on doing her best, was surprised when Miss Johnson sent Phoebe to the doors to put up the 'Closed' sign and usher the dawdlers out.

Emma was on her knees, collecting up some books someone had dropped on the floor, when there was a sudden commotion at the door and the man from the baker's shop strode in.

Miss Johnson looked up. She said severely, 'We are closed, Doctor,' but she smiled as she spoke.

'*Rupert Bear*—have you a copy? The bookshop's closed and small William next door won't go to sleep until he's read to. It must be *Rupert Bear*.' He smiled at Miss Johnson, and Emma, watching from the floor, could see Miss Johnson melting under it.

'Emma, fetch *Rupert Bear* from the last shelf in the children's section.'

As Emma got to her feet he turned and looked at her.

'Well, well,' he said softly, and his stare was just as intent as it had been in the baker's shop.

She found it disturbing, so that when she came back with the book she said tartly, 'May I have your library ticket?'

'Have I got one? Even if I knew where it was I wouldn't have stopped to get it, not with small William bawling his head off.'

He took the book from her, thanked Miss Johnson and was off.

Emma set the books neatly in their places and hoped that someone would say something. It was Phoebe who spoke.

'The poor man. I bet he's had a busy day, and now he's got to spend his evening reading to a small boy. As though he hadn't enough on his plate...'

Miss Johnson said repressively, 'He is clearly devoted to children. Emma, make a note that the book hasn't been checked out. Dr van Dyke will return it in due course.'

Well, reflected Emma, at least I know who he is. And on the way home, as she and Phoebe walked as far as the main street she asked, 'Is he the only doctor here?'

'Lord, no. There's three of them at the medical practice, and he's not permanent, just taken over from Dr Finn for a few months.'

Why had he stared so, and why had he said, 'Well, well,' in that satisfied voice? wondered Emma, saying goodnight and going back home through the quiet town.

It wouldn't be quiet for much longer. Visitors were beginning to trickle in, most of them coming ashore from their yachts, mingling with those who came regularly early in the season, to walk the coastal paths and spend leisurely days strolling through the town. More restaurants had opened, the ice cream parlour had opened its doors, and the little coastal ferry had begun its regular trips.

Emma was pleased to see that her mother was already starting to enjoy what social life there was. She played bridge regularly with Mrs Craig and her friends, met them for coffee and occasionally did some shopping. But her gentle complaints made it clear that life in a small, off-the-beaten-track town was something she was bravely enduring, and whenever Emma pointed out that there was little chance of them ever leaving the cottage, Mrs Dawson dissolved into gentle tears.

'You should have married Derek,' she said tearfully. 'We could have lived comfortably at his house. It was large enough for me to have had my own apartment...'

A remark Emma found hard to answer.

As for Emma, she hadn't much time to repine; there was the cottage to clean, the washing and the ironing, all the small household chores which she had never had to do... At first her mother had said that she would do all the shopping, but, being unused to doing this on an economical scale, it had proved quite disastrous to the household purse, so Emma had added that to her other chores. Not that she minded. She was soon on friendly terms with the shopkeepers and there was a certain satisfaction in buying groceries with a strict eye on economy instead of lifting the phone and giving the order Mrs Dawson had penned each week with a serene disregard for expense...

And Miss Johnson had unbent very slightly, pleased to find that Emma really enjoyed her work at the library. She had even had a chat about her own taste in books, deploring the lack of interest in most of the borrowers for what she called a 'good class of book'. As for Phoebe, who did her work in a cheerful slapdash fashion, Emma liked her and listened sympathetically whenever Phoebe found the time to tell her of her numerous boyfriends.

But Mrs Brooke-Tigh didn't unbend. Emma

was doing a menial's job, therefore she was treated as such; she checked the cottages with an eagle eye but beyond a distant nod had nothing to say. Emma didn't mind the cleaning but she did not like Mrs Brooke-Tigh; once the season was over she would look around for another job, something where she might meet friendly people. In a bar? she wondered, having very little idea of what that would be like. But at least there would be people and she might meet someone.

Did Dr van Dyke go into pubs? she wondered. Probably not. He wouldn't have time. She thought about him, rather wistfully, from time to time, when she was tired and lonely for the company of someone her own age. The only way she would get to know him was to get ill. And she never got ill...

Spring was sliding into early summer; at the weekends the narrow streets were filled by visiting yachtsmen and family parties driving down for a breath of sea air and a meal at one of the pubs. And with them, one Sunday, came Derek.

Mrs Dawson was going out to lunch with one of her bridge friends, persuaded that Emma didn't mind being on her own. 'We will go to evensong together,' said her mother, 'but it is such a treat to have luncheon with people I like, dear, and I knew you wouldn't mind.'

She peered at herself in the mirror. 'Is this hat all right? I really need some new clothes.'

'You look very smart, Mother, and the hat's just right. Have a lovely lunch. I'll have tea ready around four o'clock.'

Alone, Emma went into the tiny courtyard beyond the kitchen and saw to the tubs of tulips and the wallflowers growing against the wall. She would have an early lunch and go for a walk—a long walk. North Sands, perhaps, and if the little kiosk by the beach there was open she would have a cup of coffee. She went back into the cottage as someone banged the door knocker.

Derek stood there, dressed very correctly in a blazer and cords, Italian silk tie and beautifully polished shoes. For a split second Emma had a vivid mental picture of an elderly sweater and uncombed hair.

'What on earth are you doing here?' she wanted to know with a regrettable lack of delight.

Derek gave her a kind smile. He was a worthy young man with pleasant manners and had become accustomed to being liked and respected.

He said now, 'I've surprised you...'

'Indeed you have.' Emma added reluctantly. 'You'd better come in.'

Derek looked around him. 'A nice little place—rather different from Richmond, though. Has your mother settled down?'

'Yes. Why are you here?'

'I wanted to see you, Emma. To talk. If you would change into a dress we could have lunch—I'm staying at the other end of the town.'

'We can talk here. I'll make cheese sandwiches…'

'My dear girl, you deserve more than a cheese sandwich. We can talk over lunch at the hotel.'

'What about?'

'Something which will please you…'

Perhaps something they hadn't known anything about had been salvaged from her father's estate… She said slowly, 'Very well. You'll have to wait while I change, though, and I must be back before four o'clock. Mother's out to lunch.'

While she changed out of trousers and a cotton top into something suitable to accompany Derek's elegance, she wondered what he had come to tell her. Mr Trump had hinted when they had left their home that eventually there might be a little more money. Perhaps Derek had brought it with him.

When she went downstairs he was standing by the window, watching the people strolling along the path.

'Of course you can't possibly stay here. This poky little place—nothing to do all day.'

She didn't bother to answer him, and he said impatiently, 'We shall have to walk; I left the car at the hotel.'

They walked, saying little. 'I can't think why you can't tell me whatever it is at once,' said Emma.

'In good time.' They got out of the road onto the narrow pavement to allow a car to creep past. Dr van Dyke was sitting in it. If he saw her he gave no sign.

The hotel was full. They had drinks in the bar and were given a table overlooking the estuary, but Derek ignored the magnificent view while he aired his knowledge with the wine waiter.

I should be enjoying myself, reflected Emma, and I'm not.

Derek talked about his work, mutual friends she had known, the new owner of her old home.

Emma polished off the last of her trifle. 'Are you staying here on holiday?'

'No, I must return tomorrow.'

'Then you'd better tell me whatever it is.' She glanced at the clock. 'It's half past two…'

He gave a little laugh. 'Can't get rid of me soon enough, Emma?'

He put his hand over hers on the table. 'Dear Emma, I have given much thought to this. The scandal of your father's bankruptcy has died down; there are no debts, no need for people to rake over cold ashes. There is no likelihood of it hindering my career. I have come to ask you to marry me. I know you have no money and a difficult social position, but I flatter myself that I can provide both of these for my wife. In a few years the whole unfortunate matter will be forgotten. I have the deepest regard for you and you will, I know, make me an excellent wife.'

Emma had listened to this speech without moving or uttering a sound. She was so angry that she felt as though she would explode or burst into flames. She got to her feet, a well brought up young woman who had been reared to good manners and politeness whatever the circumstances.

'Get stuffed,' said Emma, and walked out of the restaurant, through the bar and swing doors and into the car park.

She was white with rage and shaking, and heedless of where she was walking. Which was why she bumped into Dr van Dyke's massive chest.

She stared up into his placid face. 'The worm, the miserable rat,' she raged. 'Him and his precious career...'

The doctor said soothingly, 'This rat, is he still in the hotel? You don't wish to meet him again?'

'If I were a man I'd knock him down...' She sniffed and gulped and two tears slid down her cheeks.

'Then perhaps it would be a good idea if you were to sit in my car for a time—in case he comes looking for you. And, if you would like to, tell me what has upset you.'

He took her arm and walked her to the car. He popped her inside and got in beside her. 'Have a good cry if you want to, and then I'll drive you home.'

He gave her a large handkerchief and sat patiently while she sniffed and snuffled and presently blew her nose and mopped her face. He didn't look at her, he was watching a man—presumably the rat—walking up and down the car park, looking around him. Presently he went back into the hotel and the doctor said, 'He's a snappy dresser, your rat.'

She sat up straight. 'He's gone? He didn't see me?'

'No.' The doctor settled back comfortably. 'What has he done to upset you? It must have been something very upsetting to cause you to leave Sunday lunch at this hotel.'

'I'd finished,' said Emma, 'and it's kind of you to ask but it's—it's...'

'None of my business. Quite right, it isn't. I'll drive you home. Where do you live?'

'The end cottage along Victoria Quay. But I can walk. It is at the end of Main Street and you can't drive there.'

He didn't answer but backed the car and turned and went out of the car park and drove up the narrow road to the back of the town. It was a very long way round and he had to park by the pub.

As he stopped Emma said, 'Thank you. I hope I haven't spoilt your afternoon.'

It would hardly do to tell her that he was enjoying every minute of it. 'I'll walk along with you, just in case the rat has got there first.'

'Do you think he has? I mean, I don't suppose he'll want to se me again.' She sniffed. 'I certainly don't want to see him.'

The doctor got out of the car and opened her door. It was a splendid car, she noticed, a dark blue Rolls-Royce, taking up almost all the space before the pub.

'You have a nice car,' said Emma, feeling

that she owed him something more than thanks.
And then blushed because it had been a silly
thing to say. Walking beside him, she reflected
that although she had wanted to meet him she
could have wished for other circumstances.

Her mother wasn't home and Emma heaved
a sigh of relief. Explaining to her mother would
be better done later on.

The doctor took the key from her and opened
the door, then stood looking at her. Mindful of
her manners she asked, 'Would you like a cup
of tea? Or perhaps you want to go back to the
hotel—someone waiting for you…?'

She was beginning to realise that he never
answered a question unless he wanted to, and
when he said quietly that he would like a cup
of tea she led the way into the cottage.

'Do sit down,' said Emma. 'I'll put the kettle
on.' And at the same time run a comb through
her mop of hair and make sure that her face
didn't look too frightful…

It was tear-stained and pale and in need of
powder and lipstick, but that couldn't be helped.
She put the kettle on, laid a tray, found the cake
tin and made the tea. When she went back into
the sitting room he was standing in front of a
watercolour of her old home.

'Your home?' he wanted to know.

'Until a month or so ago. Do you take milk and sugar?'

He sat down and took the cup and saucer she was offering him. 'Do you want to talk about the—er—rat? None of my business, of course, but doctors are the next best thing to priests when one wishes to give vent to strong feelings.'

Emma offered cake. 'You have been very kind, and I'm so grateful. But there's nothing—that is, he'll go back to London and I can forget him.'

'Of course. Do you enjoy your work at the library?'

She was instantly and unreasonably disappointed that he hadn't shown more interest or concern. She said stiffly, 'Yes, very much. Miss Johnson tells me that you don't live here, that you are filling in for another doctor?'

'Yes, I shall be sorry to leave...'

'Not yet?'

His heavy-lidded eyes gleamed. 'No, no. I'm looking forward to the summer here.' He put down his cup and saucer. 'Thank you for the tea. If you're sure there is nothing more I can do for you, I'll be off.'

Well, he had no reason to stay, thought Emma. She was hardly scintillating company.

Probably there was someone—a girl—waiting impatiently at the hotel for him.

'I hope I haven't hindered you.'

'Not in the least.'

She stood in the doorway watching him walking away, back to his car. He must think her a tiresome hysterical woman, because that was how she had behaved. And all the fault of Derek. She swallowed rage at the thought of him and went back to clear away the tea tray and lay it anew for her mother.

Mrs Dawson had had a pleasant day; she began to tell Emma about it as she came into the cottage, and it wasn't until she had had her tea and paused for breath that she noticed Emma's puffy lids and lightly pink nose.

'Emma, you've been crying. Whatever for? You never cry. You're not ill?'

'Derek came,' said Emma.

Before she could utter another word her mother cried, 'There—I knew he would. He's changed his mind, he wants to marry you—splendid; we can leave here and go back to Richmond...'

'I would not marry Derek if he was the last man on earth,' said Emma roundly. 'He said things—most unkind things—about Father...'

'You never refused him?'

'Yes, I did. He took me to lunch and I left

him at the table. I met one of the doctors from the health centre and he brought me home. Derek is a rat and a worm, and if he comes here again I shall throw something at him.'

'You must be out of your mind, Emma. Your future—our future—thrown away for no reason at all. Even if Derek upset you by speaking unkindly of your father, I'm sure he had no intention of wounding you.'

'I'm not going to marry Derek, Mother, and I hope I never set eyes on him again.'

And Emma, usually soft-hearted over her mother's whims and wishes, wouldn't discuss it any more, despite that lady's tears and gentle complaints that the miserable life she was forced to lead would send her to an early grave.

She declared that she had a headache when they got back from evensong, and retired to bed with a supper tray and a hot water bottle.

Emma pottered about downstairs, wondering if she was being selfish and ungrateful. But, even if she were, Derek was still a worm and she couldn't think how she had ever thought of marrying him.

Mrs Dawson maintained her gentle air of patient suffering for the rest of the following week, until Emma left the house on Saturday morning to clean the cottage. The week's tenants had had a large family of children and she welcomed the prospect of hard work. As indeed it was; the little place looked as though it had been hit by a cyclone. It would take all her time to get it pristine for the next family.

She set to with a will and was in the kitchen, giving everything a final wipe-down, when the cottage door opened and Mrs Brooke-Tigh came in, and with her Dr van Dyke and a pretty woman of about Emma's own age.

Mrs Brooke-Tigh ignored her. 'You're so lucky,' she declared loudly, 'that I had this last-minute cancellation. Take a quick look round and see if it will suit. The next party are due here in half an hour but the girl's almost finished.'

'The girl', scarlet-faced, had turned her back but then had to turn round again. 'Miss Dawson,' said Dr van Dyke, 'what a pleasant surprise. This is my sister, who plans to come for a week with her children.'

He turned to the woman beside him. 'Wibeke, this is Emma Dawson; she lives here.'

Emma wiped a soapy hand on her pinny and shook hands, wishing herself anywhere else but there, and listened to Wibeke saying how pleased she was to meet her while Mrs Brooke-Tigh, at a loss for words for once, tapped an impatient foot.

Presently she led them away to see round the

cottage, and when they were on the point of leaving Mrs Brooke-Tigh said loudly, 'I'll be back presently to pay you, Emma. Leave the cleaning things at my back door as you go.'

The perfect finish for a beastly week, thought Emma, grinding her splendid teeth.

And Mrs Brooke-Tigh hardly improved matters when she paid Emma.

'It doesn't do to be too familiar with the tenants,' she pointed out. 'I hardly think it necessary to tell you that. Don't be late on Wednesday.'

Emma, who was never late, bade her good afternoon in a spine-chilling voice and went home.

It would have been very satisfying to have tossed the bucket and mop at Mrs Brooke-Tigh and never returned, but with the bucket and mop there would have gone sixty pounds, not forgetting the tips left on the dressing table. She would have to put up with Mrs Brooke-Tigh until the season ended, and in the meantime she would keep her ears open for another job. That might mean going to Kingsbridge every day, since so many of the shops and hotels closed for the winter at Salcombe.

Too soon to start worrying, Emma told herself as she laid out some of the sixty pounds on a chicken for Sunday lunch and one of the rich creamy cakes from the patisserie which her mother enjoyed.

To make up for her horrid Saturday, Sunday was nice, warm and sunny so that she was able to wear a jersey dress, slightly out of date but elegant, and of a pleasing shade of blue. After matins, while her mother chatted with friends, a pleasant young man with an engaging smile introduced himself as Mrs Craig's son.

'Here for a few days,' he told her, and, 'I don't know a soul. Do take pity on me and show me round.'

He was friendly and she readily agreed. 'Though I have part time jobs…'

'When are you free? What about tomorrow morning?'

'I must do the shopping…'

'Splendid, I'll come with you and carry the basket. We could have coffee. Where shall I meet you?'

'At the bakery at the bottom of Main Street, about ten o'clock?'

'Right, I'll look forward to that. The name's Brian, by the way.'

'Emma,' said Emma. 'Your mother is waiting and so's mine.'

'Such a nice boy,' said her mother over lunch, and added, 'He is twenty-three, just qualified as a solicitor. He's rather young, of course...' She caught Emma's eye. 'It is a great pity that you sent Derek away.'

Emma quite liked shopping, and she enjoyed it even more with Brian to carry her basket and talk light-heartedly about anything which caught his eye. They lingered over coffee and then went back through the town to collect sausages from the butcher. His shop was next to one of the restaurants in the town and Brian paused outside it.

'This looks worth a visit. Have dinner with me one evening, Emma?'

'Not on Tuesday or Thursday; I work at the library.'

'Wednesday? Shall we meet here, inside, at half past seven.'

'I'd like that, thank you.' She smiled at him. 'Thank you for the coffee; I've enjoyed my morning.'

Miss Johnson was grumpy on Tuesday evening and Mrs Brooke-Tigh was more than usually high-handed the following day. She couldn't find fault with Emma's work, but somehow she managed to give the impression that it wasn't satisfactory. Which made the prospect of an evening out with Brian very inviting. Emma put on the jersey dress once more and went along to the restaurant.

Brian was waiting for her, obviously glad to see her, and sat her down at the small table, ordering drinks.

In reply to her enquiry as to what he thought of the town he smiled wryly. 'It's a charming little place, but after London's bright lights... What do you do with yourself all day long?'

'Me? Well, there's the library and the shopping, and all the chores, and we're beginning to know more people now.'

'You don't get bored? My mother likes living here; it's a splendid place for elderly widows: nice hotels, bridge, coffee, reading a good book in the sun, gossiping—but you are rather young for that.'

'I've been coming here ever since I was a small girl. It's a kind of a second home, although most of the people I knew have left the town. But I'm quite content.'

They went to their table and ate lobster and a complicated ice cream pudding, and finished a bottle of white wine between them, lingering over their coffee until Emma said, 'I really must go home. Mother insisted that she would wait up for me and she sleeps badly.'

'I'm going back on Friday. But I'm told there's a good pub at Hope Cove. Will you have lunch with me there? I'll pick you up around twelve-thirty?'

'Thank you, that would be nice. If you like walking we could go along the beach if the tide's out.'

'Splendid. I'll walk you back.'

They parted at the cottage door in a friendly fashion, though Emma was aware that he only sought her company because he was bored and didn't know anyone else...

Her mother was in her dressing gown, eager for an account of her evening.

'You'll go out with him again if he asks you?' she enquired eagerly.

'I'm having lunch with him on Friday.' Emma yawned and kicked off her best shoes. 'He's going back to London; I think he is bored here.'

'Mrs Craig was telling me that she wishes he would settle down...'

'Well, he won't here; that's a certainty.' Emma kissed her mother goodnight and went to bed, aware that her mother had hoped for more than a casual friendship with Brian.

He is still a boy, thought Emma sleepily, and allowed her thoughts to turn to Dr van Dyke who, she suspected, was very much a man.

Miss Johnson was still grumpy on Thursday evening, but since it was pay day Emma forgave her. Besides, she was kept busy by people wanting books for the weekend. She felt quite light-hearted as she went home, her wages in her purse, planning something tasty for the weekend which wouldn't make too large a hole in the housekeeping.

Friday was warm and sunny, and she was out early to do the weekend shopping for there would be no time on Saturday. Her mother was going out to lunch with one of her new-found friends and Emma raced around, getting everything ready for cooking the supper and, just in case Brian wanted to come back for tea, she laid a tea tray.

He came promptly and they walked through the town to the car park. He drove up the road bordering the estuary onto the main road and then turned off to Hope Cove. The road was narrow now, running through fields, with a glimpse of the sea. When they reached the tiny village and parked by the pub there were already a number of cars there.

The pub was dark and oak-beamed and low-ceilinged inside, and already quite full.

Brian looked around him. 'I like this place—full of atmosphere and plenty of life. What shall we eat?'

They had crab sandwiches, and he had a beer and Emma a glass of white wine, and since there was no hurry they sat over the food while he told her of his work.

'Of course I could never leave London,' he told her. 'I've a flat overlooking the river and any number of friends and a good job. I shall have to come and see Mother from time to time, but a week is about as much as I can stand.' He added, 'Don't you want to escape, Emma?'

'Me? Where to?'

'Mother told me that you lived in Richmond. You must have had friends...'

'My father went bankrupt,' she said quietly. 'Yes, we had friends—fair-weather friends. And we're happy here. Mother has made several new friends, so she goes out quite a lot, and I'm happy.' She went on, 'If you've finished, shall we walk along the cliff path for a while? The view is lovely...'

She hadn't been quite truthful, she reflected, but she sensed that Brian was a young man who didn't like to be made uneasy. He would go back to his flat and his friends, assuring himself that her life was just what she wanted.

They drove back to Salcombe presently, parked the car at the hotel and walked back through the town.

Outside the bakery Emma stopped. 'Don't come any further,' she suggested. 'If you are going back today I expect you want to see your mother before you go. I enjoyed lunch; Hope

Cove is a delightful little place. I hope you have a good journey back home.'

'I'll leave within the hour; it's quite a long trip. I'll be glad to get back. Life's a bit slow here, isn't it? I wish we could have seen more of each other, but I expect you'll still be here if and when I come again.'

'Oh, I expect so.' She offered a hand and he took it and kissed her cheek.

Dr van Dyke, coming round the corner, stopped short, wished them a cheerful hello and gave Emma a look to send the colour into her cheeks. It said all too clearly that she hadn't wasted much time in finding someone to take Derek's place.

He went into the baker's, and she bade a final hasty goodbye to Brian and almost ran to the cottage. The doctor would think... She didn't go too deeply into what he would think; she hoped that she wouldn't see him again for a very long time.

It was a brilliant morning on Saturday, and already warm when she got to Mrs Brooke-Tigh's house, collected her cleaning brushes and cloths and started on her chores. From a bedroom window she watched Mrs Brooke-Tigh go down the lane, swinging her beach bag. On Saturday mornings she went to the hotel at the other end of the town, which had a swimming pool and a delightful terrace where one could laze for hours. The moment she was out of sight the girl in the other cottage crossed over and came upstairs.

'Thought I'd let you know I've given in my notice. She's furious; she'll never get anyone by Wednesday. Wouldn't hurt her to do a bit of housework herself. Mind she doesn't expect you to take on any more work.'

Emma was stripping beds. 'I don't see how she can...'

'She'll think of something. I'd better get on, I suppose. Bye.'

Mrs Brooke-Tigh came back earlier than usual; Emma was setting the tea tray ready for the next tenants when she walked in.

'That girl's leaving,' she told Emma without preamble. 'She never was much good but at least she was a pair of hands. I'll never get anyone else at such short notice. We will have to manage as best we can. I shall notify the next two weeks' tenants that they can't come in until six o'clock. If you come at nine o'clock and work until six you can do both cottages. I'll pay you another fifteen pounds a day—thirty pounds a week more.'

Emma didn't answer at once. The money would be useful... 'I'm willing to do that for the next week and, if I must, the second week. But no longer than that.'

Mrs Brooke-Tigh sniffed. 'I should have thought that you would have jumped at the chance of more money.' She would have said more, but the look Emma gave her left the words dying on her tongue. Instead she said ungraciously, 'Well, all right, I'll agree to that.' She turned to go. 'Bring your stuff over and I'll pay you.'

There was a car outside the door as she left. It appeared to be full of small children, and a friendly young woman, the one who had been with the doctor, got out. 'I say, hello, how nice to meet you again. We're here for a week so we must get to know each other.' She smiled. 'Where's that woman who runs the place?'

'I'll fetch her,' said Emma, 'and I'd love to see you again.'

CHAPTER THREE

IT WAS quite late in the evening when the phone rang. 'It's me, Wibeke Wolff. There wasn't time to talk so I got that woman to give me your phone number. I do know who you are, Roele told me, so please forgive me for ringing you up. I don't know anyone here. Roele's only free occasionally, and I wondered if you would show me the best places to take the children. A beach where they can be safe in the water? If you would like, could we go somewhere tomorrow? I'll get a picnic organised. This is awful cheek...'

'I'd love a picnic,' said Emma. 'There are some lovely beaches but we don't need to go far tomorrow; there's South Sands only a few minutes in a car. Would that do for a start?'

'It sounds ideal. You're sure you don't mind?'

'No, of course not. Where shall I meet you?'

'Here at this cottage? About ten o'clock? I thought we might come back about three o'clock. You're sure I'm not spoiling your day?'

'No, I'm looking forward to it. And I'll be there in the morning.'

'Who was that, Emma?' Her mother looked hopeful. 'Someone you have met taking you out for lunch?'

'A picnic. Mrs Wibeke Wolff with three children; we're having a picnic lunch at South Sands tomorrow.'

'Oh, well, I suppose it's a change for you. I shall be out in the afternoon; I'll make a sandwich or something for my lunch.'

Emma took this remark for what it was worth. Her mother had no intention of doing any such thing. She said cheerfully, 'I'll leave lunch all ready for you, Mother, and cook supper after we've been to church. Unless you want to go to Matins?'

'You know I need my rest in the morning. Just bring me a cup of tea and I'll manage my own breakfast.'

'If you want to,' said Emma briskly. 'There'll be breakfast as usual in the morning, but if you would rather get up later and cook something?'

'No, no, I'll come down in my dressing gown. I don't have much strength in the morning, but then of course I have always been delicate.'

Emma, her head full of the morrow's picnic, wasn't listening.

Sunday was another glorious morning. Emma got into a cotton dress and sandals, found a straw hat and a swimsuit, got breakfast for her gently complaining parent and made her way through the still quiet streets to the holiday cottages.

Wibeke was loading the car and waved a greeting. As Emma reached her she said, 'I've got the children inside. Everyone here seems to be asleep and they're noisy.'

Emma glanced at Mrs Brooke-Tigh's house. There was no sign of life there and the curtains were still drawn. A good thing, since she didn't approve of the cleaners mixing with the tenants. Emma said, 'Hello, it's going to be a warm day; the beach will be pretty crowded.'

'The children will love that.' Wibeke opened the door and they piled out. 'Hetty, George and Rosie,' said Wibeke as Emma shook hands with them. They were three small excited kids, bursting with impatience to get their day on the beach started. Without waste of time they crowded into the back of the car and, with Emma beside her, Wibeke drove through the town and along the coast road. It was a short drive.

'It's really only a short walk away,' said

Emma as they began the business of parking the car and unloading the children and picnic basket, the buckets and spades, the swimsuits...

The beach was full but not crowded. They settled against some rocks and got into their swimsuits, and Wibeke and the children raced to the water's edge while Emma guarded their belongings. It was pleasant sitting there, for the sun was warm but not yet hot enough to be uncomfortable, and there was no one near by. This, she reflected, was the first day out she had had since they'd come to Salcombe. She didn't count Derek or Brian, for she hadn't been at ease with either of them, but Wibeke and the children were friendly and undemanding; she had only just met them and yet she felt that she had known Wibeke for years. Of course they would all be gone in a week, but still she would have pleasant memories...

They came trooping back and Wibeke said, 'It's your turn now. A pity we can't all go together. Do you suppose we might? There's no one very close and we could see our belongings easily...'

'Let's wait and see if the beach fills up.'

The water was chilly, but within seconds Emma was swimming strongly away from the beach and then idling on her back until the thought of Wibeke coping with three small children sent her back again.

Time passed, as it always did when one was happy, far too quickly. They built sandcastles, dug holes and filled them with buckets of water, and went swimming again. This time Wibeke stayed on the beach.

Wibeke was peering into the picnic basket when Dr van Dyke joined her.

'Roele, how lovely. Have you come to lunch? You're wearing all the wrong clothes.'

'I've been to see a patient and I've another call to make; no one is going to take advice from a man in swimming trunks.' He was watching the children and Emma prancing around at the water's edge, her magnificent shape enhanced by her simple swimsuit, her bright hair tied up untidily on the top of her head.

'She's rather gorgeous, isn't she?' Wibeke peeped at her brother. 'She should be out in the fashionable world, with a string of boyfriends and lovely clothes.'

'Never.'

The doctor spoke so emphatically that she stared at him, and then smiled.

'Why, Roele...'

But by then the bathing party were within a few feet of them, and while the children rushed at their uncle Emma hung back, taken by surprise, feeling suddenly shy.

'Hello,' said the doctor easily. 'I see you've been landed with these tiresome brats—sandcastles and looking for crabs and digging holes—you'll be exhausted. Don't let them bully you.' He got up, the children clinging to him. 'I must go—have a lovely day and don't get too much sun.'

He hadn't really looked at her, she reflected, just a casual smile and a wave as he went. She had been silly to feel shy.

By mid-afternoon the children were tired, and they left the now crowded beach and drove back to the cottage.

'Come in and have a cup of tea,' begged Wibeke, but Emma shook her head.

'It's been a lovely day but I really must go home. If you would like me to babysit one evening I'll do that gladly. It'll give you a change to go out if you want to.'

'Would you really? That would be great. What are you doing tomorrow?'

'Shopping, washing, ironing, household chores—but would you all like to come to tea? We're right by the water and there's lots for the children to see.'

'We'd like that. Where exactly do you live?'

Emma told her, bade the sleepy children goodbye, and went home.

Her mother was there, complaining in her gentle voice that it had been far too warm at the hotel, where she had had tea with Mrs Craig. 'I'm not sure that I have the energy to go to evensong.'

'You'll feel better when I've made another cup of tea—China, with a slice of lemon.'

'You enjoyed your day?' asked her mother.

'Very much. The sea's a bit chilly but it was lovely to swim... I've invited Mrs Wolff and the children to tea tomorrow. You might enjoy meeting them.'

'Small children? Emma, dear, you know how quickly I get a headache if there's too much noise, and children are so noisy.'

'You'd like Wibeke—Mrs Wolff...'

'Shall I? How did you meet?'

Emma had glossed over her second job; her mother would have been horrified to know that she was doing someone else's housework. 'Oh,' she said vaguely, 'she is staying for a week in a rented cottage.'

There was no need to say more for her mother had lost interest.

As it turned out, the tea party was a success. Wibeke was a lively talker, full of the light-hearted gossip Mrs Dawson enjoyed, and willing to discuss the latest fashions, the newest plays and films, who was marrying whom and who was getting divorced. When she and the children had gone, Mrs Dawson pronounced her to be a very nice young woman.

'Obviously married well and leading a pleasant social life.' She looked reproachfully at Emma as she spoke. 'Just as you would have if you hadn't been so foolish about Derek.' And when Emma didn't reply she added, 'I must say the children were quiet.'

Well, of course they were, reflected Emma, who had made it her business to keep them occupied—first with a good tea and then with a visit to her bedroom, where they had been allowed to open cupboards and drawers, try on her hats and shoes while George took the books from her bookshelf and piled them in neat heaps. For a three-year-old he was a bright child, so she had hugged him and told him that he was a clever boy, and that had led to hugs for the little girls, too. She felt a stab of envy of Wibeke...

The doctor called on his sister in the late evening.

She gave him a drink and sat down opposite him in the little living room.

'We all went to Emma's cottage and had tea.

Have you met her mother? Darling, she's a ball and chain round Emma's neck. Charming, small and dainty and wistful, harping on about having to live here after an obviously comfortable life at Richmond. Told me that Emma had chosen to reject some man or other who wanted to marry her.'

The doctor smiled. 'Ah, yes, the rat…'

Wibeke sat up. 'You know about him? Have you met him?'

'I happened to be handy at the time. He would never have done for Emma.'

'Perhaps she will meet a man here, though she doesn't have much of a social life. Not that she says much; it's what she doesn't say…'

'Quite. Is Harry coming down on Saturday to see you back home?'

This was a change of conversation not to be ignored. 'Yes, bless him. He'll take George and most of the luggage, and I'll have the girls. We plan to leave quite early.' She peeped at the doctor. 'Before Emma starts her cleaning.'

And if she had expected an answer to that, she didn't get it.

When Emma got to the cottages in the morning there was a good deal of bustle. The children, reluctant to go, were being stowed into their mother's car, and Wibeke was fastening George into his seat behind his father, who was packing in the luggage.

'We're off,' cried Wibeke as soon as she saw Emma. 'This is Harry. Come and say hello and goodbye!'

Which Emma did, uncaring of the fact that she would be late starting her day's cleaning and sorry to see them go. She had liked Wibeke and Wibeke had liked her; they could have been friends...

The little lane seemed very quiet when they had driven away, as Emma fetched her bucket and brushes and started work.

It was a scramble to be finished by six o'clock, and the second lot of tenants drove up as she closed the door. She had managed to get one cottage ready in time for the early arrival of its occupants, but she told herself that, despite the extra money, one more week of doing two persons' work was all she intended to do.

She told Mrs Brooke-Tigh that when she stowed away her cleaning things.

'You young women are all the same,' said Mrs Brooke-Tigh nastily. 'Do as little as you can get away with for as much as possible.'

'Well,' said Emma sweetly, 'if you cleaned two of the cottages you would only need to find one young woman.'

Mrs Brooke-Tigh gave her a look of horrified

indignation. Emma didn't give her a chance to reply but wished her good evening and went home. She was tired and, not only that, she was dispirited; the future, as far as she could see, was uninviting. The pleasant hours she had spent with Wibeke and the children had made that clear.

As though that wasn't bad enough, she was met by her mother's excited admission that she had seen the most charming dress at the boutique. 'Such a sweet colour, palest blue—you know how that suits me, dear—I just had to have it. I've not had anything new for months. When your dear father was alive he never grudged me anything.'

Emma took off her shoes from her aching feet. 'Mother, Father had money; we haven't— only just enough to keep us going. How much was the dress?'

Her mother pouted. 'I knew you'd make a fuss.' She began to weep tears of self-pity. 'And to think that everything could have been so different if only you hadn't sent Derek away.'

Too tired to argue, Emma went to the kitchen to start the supper, and while she cooked it she drank a mug of very strong tea—a bottle of brandy would have been nice, or champagne. In fact anything which would drown her feeling of frustration. Something would have to be done, but what? Her mother had made up her mind to be unhappy at Salcombe; she had always taken it for granted that anything she wanted she could have and she had made no attempt to understand that that was no longer possible. If only something would happen...

She was coming out of the bakery on Monday morning when she met Dr van Dyke going in. He wasted no time on polite greetings. 'The very person I wanted to see. Wait while I get my pasties.'

Outside the shop, Emma asked, 'Why do you fetch pasties? Haven't you got a housekeeper or someone to look after you?'

'Yes, yes, of course I have, but when I have a visit at one of the outlying farms I take my lunch with me. Don't waste time asking silly questions. One of my partners is unexpectedly short of a receptionist and general dogsbody. No time to go to an agency or advertise. He's a bit desperate. Would you care to take on the job, Monday to Friday, until he can get things sorted out? Half past eight until eleven o'clock, then five in the afternoon until half past six.'

She stood gaping at him. 'You really mean it? Would I really do?'

'I don't see why not; you seem a sensible girl. Oh, and there's no evening surgery on Tuesdays and Thursdays.'

'So I could still work at the library?'

'Yes. Come up to the surgery after eleven o'clock and see Dr Walters. Talk it over with him.'

He nodded goodbye and strode away. Emma watched him go, not quite believing any of it but knowing that after eleven o'clock she would be at the surgery, doing her best to look like a suitable applicant for the post of receptionist.

She did the rest of the shopping in a hopeful haze, hurried home to tidy her unruly hair and get into her less scruffy sandals, told her mother that she would be back for lunch and made her way through the town.

The surgery was at the back of the town, away from the main street. It was pleasantly situated in a quiet street, and even if the surgery hours were over it was still busy. Bidden to wait, since Dr Walters was seeing his last patient, Emma sat down in the waiting room and whiled away ten minutes or so leafing through out-of-date copies of country magazines, at the same time rehearsing the kind of replies she might be expected to give. Since she had no idea of the questions she would be asked, it was a fruitless occupation.

The moment she entered Dr Walters's surgery she knew that she need not have worried. He was a small middle-aged man, with the kind of trustful face which made women want to mother him. He was also a very good doctor, though untidy, and forgetful of anything which wasn't connected with his work or his patients. His desk was an untidy mass of papers, patients' notes, various forms and a pile of unopened letters.

He got up as she went in, dislodging papers and knocking over a small pot full of pens.

'Miss Dawson.' He came round the desk to shake hands. 'Dr van Dyke told me that you might consider helping out—my receptionist and secretary, Mrs Crump, had to leave at a moment's notice—her daughter has had an accident. She will return, of course, but I need help until she does.'

He waved Emma to a chair and went back behind the desk. 'Have you any experience of this type of work?'

'None at all—' there was no point in pretending otherwise '—but I can answer the telephone, file papers, sort out the post, make appointments and usher patients in and out.'

Dr Walters peered at her over his old-fashioned spectacles. 'You're honest. Shall we give it a trial? I'm desperate for help with the paperwork. I can't pay you the usual salary because you aren't trained. Could we settle for—

let me see...' He named a sum which made Emma blink.

'I'm not worth that much,' she told him, 'but I'd like the job.'

'It's yours until Mrs Crump gets back. If after a week I think that you don't deserve the money I'll reduce it. No references—Dr van Dyke seems to know enough about you. Start tomorrow? Half past eight? We'll see how we get on.'

For all his mild appearance, Emma reflected, he certainly knew his own mind.

The next few months were the happiest Emma had spent since her father died. She sorted patients' notes from letters, and letters from the endless junk mail, she kept the doctor's desk tidy, and saw that the day's patients were clearly listed and laid on his blotter where he couldn't possibly mislay the list, she answered the phone and booked patients in and out. She didn't attempt to do any of Mrs Crump's skilled jobs, and she had no doubt that that lady would have a great deal of work to deal with when she returned, but she did her best and Dr Walters, once he realised her limitations, made no complaint.

And in all that time she barely glimpsed Dr van Dyke. A brief good morning if they should meet at the surgery, a wave of the hand if she passed him on her way home… She told herself that there was no reason for him to do more than acknowledge her, but all the same she was disappointed.

All the wrong men like me, she thought crossly, and when I do meet a man I would like to know better he ignores me.

The season was at its height when Mrs Dawson received an invitation to go and stay with an elderly couple who had been friendly with her and her husband before his death. The friendship had cooled, but now it seemed that sufficient time had glossed over the unfortunate circumstances following his death and they expressed themselves delighted at the prospect of a visit from her.

'So kind,' declared Mrs Dawson. 'Of course I shall accept! How delightful it will be to go back to the old life, even if it is only for a few weeks. You will be able to manage on your own, won't you, Emma? You are so seldom home these days, and although I'm sure you don't mean to neglect me I am sometimes lonely. There is so little to do,' she added peevishly.

There were several answers to that, but Emma uttered none of them.

'I shall be perfectly all right, Mother. You'll enjoy the change, won't you? When do they want you to go? We must see about travelling. Someone will meet you at Paddington?'

'Yes, I couldn't possibly manage on my own. I shall need some new clothes...'

Emma thought of the small nest egg at the bank. 'I'm sure we can manage something; you have some pretty dresses...'

'Last year's,' snapped her mother. 'Everyone will recognise them.' She added, 'After all, you take half my pension each week.'

They mustn't quarrel, thought Emma. 'You will have all of it while you are away,' she pointed out gently, 'and we'll put our heads together about some new clothes for you.'

'I must say that since your father died, Emma, you have become very bossy and mean. I suppose it's the result of living here in this poky little cottage with no social life.'

'Now I'm working at the medical centre I haven't much time to be sociable. And, Mother, we couldn't manage unless I had a job. When do you plan to go?'

'On Friday. I'll collect my pension on Thursday; that will give me a little money in my purse. I want to go to the boutique tomorrow and see if there is anything that I can afford.' She looked at Emma. 'How much money can I spend?'

When Emma told her, she said, 'Not nearly enough, but I suppose I'll have to manage.'

A most unsatisfactory conversation, thought Emma, lying in bed and doing sums in her head that night. Mrs Crump wasn't going to stay at home for ever. Sooner or later she would lose her job, and with summer coming to an end so would the kind of jobs she could apply for. Of course she could live more cheaply when her mother had gone, but once summer was over there would be the cottage to keep warm and lighted.

She shook up her pillows again, determined to think of something else. And that wasn't at all satisfactory, for all she could think about was the complete lack of interest in her envinced by Dr van Dyke.

Mrs Dawson spent a good deal more money than Emma had bargained for. There had been such a splendid choice, her mother enthused, and really the prices were so reasonable it would have been foolish to ignore such bargains. At least she was happy getting ready for her visit, talking about nothing else.

Emma, tidying books on the library shelves, listening to Phoebe's cheerful gossip, thought about her day with Dr Walters. He had been untidier than usual, and his morning patients had taken longer than usual too. It had been almost one o'clock before she had been ready to leave, and then she had discovered his scribbled note asking her to return for an hour that afternoon as he had arranged to see a patient privately.

She had hurried home, got lunch and rushed to the shops with her Mother's wispy voice echoing in her ears; there was so much to tell her about the letter she had received from her friends and Emma couldn't be bothered to stay and listen. Emma, racing in and out of the butcher, the greengrocer and the bakery, prayed for patience…!

Getting her mother away on time, properly packed and the journey made as easy as possible, hadn't been the problem she had feared. Mrs Craig had offered to drive her mother to Totnes to catch the train, and the prospect of leaving Salcombe had changed her from a disgruntled woman to a charming lady who, having got what she wanted, was prepared to be nice to everyone. All the same Emma, who loved her mother, missed her.

Life became more leisurely as there was less of everything to do: meals didn't need to be on time, the cottage, with only her in it, was easy to keep clean and tidy, and it no longer mattered if she needed to stay late at the surgery.

Her mother was happy too; she had met several old friends, all of whom wanted her to visit them. 'I shan't be home yet,' she told Emma gleefully. Emma, relieved to know that her mother was once more living the life she enjoyed, permitted herself to forget the worries of the forthcoming winter. The summer was sliding gently into autumn, and although there were still plenty of visitors very soon now the shops would close for the winter. And still there was no news of Mrs Crump's return...

Her mother had been gone for two weeks when Dr Walters, sipping coffee after the morning surgery, began tossing the papers on his desk all over the place. He found what he wanted, a letter, and he put on his glasses.

'News, Emma. I have heard from Mrs Crump. She at last sees her way clear to returning to work.' He glanced at the letter. 'In a week's time. That brings us to Friday, which is most convenient for there is no surgery on Saturday, so you will be able to leave after Friday evening surgery.'

He beamed at her across the desk. 'I must say I shall be sorry to see you go; you have been of great help to me. I'm sure I don't know how I would have managed without you. You will be glad to be free again, no doubt?'

'Yes,' said Emma steadily, 'that will be nice, Dr Walters, although I have enjoyed working here for you. I expect Mrs Crump will be delighted to come back to work and you will be equally pleased to have her.'

'Indeed, I shall.' He put down his cup. 'I must be off. I'll leave you to clear up and I'll see you this evening.'

Emma set about putting the place to rights, her thoughts chaotic. She should have been prepared for the news but she had been lulled by several weeks of silence from Mrs Crump so that leaving had become a comfortably vague event which she didn't need to be worried about just yet. She would have to set about finding another job, for her hours at the library would hardly keep body and soul together.

She finished her chores and left the medical centre just as Dr van Dyke got out of his car. For once he stopped to speak to her.

'Rather late leaving, aren't you? Not being overworked, are you?'

'No, no, thank you.' She tried to think of something casual to say, but her mind was blank and at any moment now she was going to burst into tears.

'I must hurry,' she told him, and almost ran down the road.

He stood watching her fast retreating back, frowning; he had been careful to avoid her during the past months, aware that she attracted him and just as aware that he would be returning to Holland within a few weeks and that to allow the attraction to grow would be foolhardy. Perhaps it was a good thing that she showed no signs of even liking him.

He went along to his surgery and forgot about her. But later that evening he allowed his thoughts to return to her, smiling a little at her rage at the hotel and then again at the quite different Emma, playing with the children on the sands.

Back at the cottage, Emma gave way to her feelings. The situation called for a good cry, not a gentle flow of tears easily wiped away with a dainty hanky and a few sighs. She sat bawling her eyes out, her face awash, sniffing and snuffling and wiping away the tears with her hands, catching her breath like a child. It was a great relief, and presently she found a hanky and mopped her face and felt better. It was something which she had known would happen, and she told herself that it wasn't the end of the world; she would soon find another job—probably not as well paid, but enough to live on. It was a good thing that her mother was away...

She washed her sodden face, tidied her hair and made a sandwich and a pot of tea, and, not wishing to show her red nose and puffy lids to the outside world, spent the afternoon doing the ironing. By the time it was necessary to go back to work she was almost herself again, fortified by yet more tea and careful repairs to her face.

There were a lot of patients, and Dr Walters was far too busy to do more than glance at her. Confident that she looked exactly as usual, she ushered patients in and out, found notes and made herself generally useful. Only to come face to face with Dr van Dyke.

She tried sidling past him and found her arm gently held.

'So you will be leaving us, Emma. Dr Walters is sorry to see you go, but I dare say you will be glad of more leisure?'

'Oh, I shall, I shall… I can't stop. Dr Walters wants some notes.'

He took his hand away and she skipped off to hide behind a cupboard door until he had gone. The less she saw of him the better, she told herself, and knew that that wasn't true. But he would be gone in a few weeks and she would forget him.

The week went too rapidly, and her last day came. She said goodbye to everyone—everyone except Dr van Dyke, who had gone across the estuary to East Portlemouth to deliver a baby.

'You're bound to see him around the town

before he leaves,' observed Dr Walters. 'We shall miss him, but of course he wants to go back to his own practice, and naturally we shall all be glad to see Dr Finn back again. Probably he will bring back a number of new ideas from the States.'

There was a letter from her mother when she got home; she wouldn't be coming home for the next week or so, she wrote.

And Alice Riddley—remember her, my old schoolfriend—has made an exciting suggestion to me, but I will let you know more about that later, when we have discussed it thoroughly. I'm sure you are enjoying yourself without your tiresome old mother to look after. Make lots of young friends, Emma, and buy yourself some pretty dresses. You can afford them now that I'm not at home to buy food for.

Emma folded the letter carefully. Why was it that her mother always made her feel guilty? As for new clothes, every penny would need to be hoarded until she had more work. She would start looking on Monday...

Mrs Craig stopped her after church on Sunday. 'I have had a letter from your mother;

she hints at all kinds of exciting happenings for the future. Do you know what she means, dear?'

'No, I've no idea, Mrs Craig. She mentioned that she would have something to tell me later, but I've no idea what it is. She won't be coming home for another week or two.'

'You're not lonely, Emma?'

'Not a bit; the days are never long enough...'

A pity she couldn't say the same of the nights. Why is it, she wondered, that one's brain is needle-sharp around three o'clock in the morning, allowing one to make impossible plans, do complicated mental arithmetic and see the future in a pessimistic light?

She started her job-hunting on the Monday. The season was coming to an end, temporary jobs would finish very soon, and since so many of the shops would shut until the spring there was no question of them taking on more staff. The holiday cottages to rent would lock their doors and the few for winter-letting were maintained by their owners.

After several days Emma realised that she would have to go to Kingsbridge and find work there. It would mean a daily bus ride, and not much leisure, but if she could find something full-time that would see them through the winter. There was a large supermarket there which sounded promising...

She had seen nothing of Dr van Dyke. Perhaps he had already left, she wondered, and found the thought depressed her. He might not have liked her but she would have liked to have known him better. And he had been very kind about Derek.

She went to the library on Thursday evening, and as they packed up Miss Johnson called her over. 'After this week we shall be closing down the evening session and I'm afraid there won't be enough work for you to continue, Emma. We shall be sorry to let you go but there wouldn't be anything for you to do. If you would come on Tuesday evening and help us go through the shelves and generally tidy up...'

Emma found her voice. It didn't sound quite like hers but at least it was steady. 'I shall miss working here. Perhaps I could come back next year? And of course I'll come on Tuesday.' She said goodnight, called a cheerful greeting to Phoebe and went home.

This was something she hadn't foreseen. The money from the library wasn't enough to live on, but it would have helped to eke out her savings until she was working again. This time she didn't cry; she hadn't time for that. She would have to plan for the next few weeks, pay one or two outstanding bills, think up some cheap menus. At least she had only herself to think about.

She was getting into bed much later when she heard a faint whine. It sounded as though it was coming from the front garden and she went downstairs to have a look, opening the door cautiously, forgetful that she was in her nightie and with bare feet.

There was a very small dog peering at her through the closed gate, and she went at once to open it. The cottage next door was empty of visitors so there was no one about. The dog crept past her and slid into the cottage, its tail between its legs, shivering.

Emma fetched a bowl of bread and milk and watched the little beast wolf it down. It was woefully thin, its coat bedraggled, and there was a cut over one eye. There was no question of sending it on its way. She fetched an old towel and rubbed the skinny little body while the dog shivered and shook under her gentle hands.

'More bread and milk?' said Emma. 'And a good night's sleep. Tomorrow I shall give you a good wash. I always wanted a dog and it seems I'm meant to have one.'

She carried him upstairs to bed then, wrapped in a towel, and he fell asleep before she had turned out the light. She went to sleep too, quite forgetful of the fact that she was out of work and, worse, was never going to see Dr van Dyke again.

CHAPTER FOUR

IT WAS raining when she woke up in the early morning and the little dog was still asleep, wrapped in the towel. But he opened frightened eyes the moment she moved and cowered away from her hand.

'My poor dear,' said Emma. 'Don't be frightened. You're going to live here and turn into a handsome dog, and in any case this is no weather to turn you out into the street.'

He pricked up his ears at her voice and wagged a wispy tail, and presently, rendered bold by the promise of breakfast, went cautiously downstairs with her.

She had intended job-hunting directly after breakfast, but that would have to wait for a while. Full of a good breakfast, the dog accepted her efforts to clean him up, sitting on his towel in the little kitchen, being washed and dried and gently brushed. When she had finished he looked more like a dog, and cautiously licked her hand as she cleaned the wound over his eye. By that time it was mid-morning and he was ready for another meal…

Emma found an old blanket, arranged it in one of the chairs, and with the aid of a biscuit urged him into it.

'I'm going out,' she told him. 'You need food and so do I.'

A marrow bone was added to the sausages for her own lunch, suitable dog food and dog biscuits and, in one of the small shops which sold everything, a collar and lead. She went back in the rain and found him asleep, but he instantly awoke when she went in, cowering down into the blanket.

She gave him another biscuit and told him that he was a brave boy, then fastened the collar round his scrawny neck and went into the garden with him and waited patiently while he pottered among the flowerbeds and then sped back indoors.

'Time for another meal,' said Emma, and opened a tin. Since he was still so frightened and cowed she stayed home for the rest of the day, and was rewarded by the lessening of his cringing fear and his obvious pleasure in his food. By bedtime he was quite ready to go upstairs with her and curl up on her feet in bed, anxious to please, looking at her with large brown eyes.

'Tomorrow,' she told him, 'I must go looking
for work, but you'll be safe here and we will
go for a little walk together and you'll learn to
be a dog again. I have no doubt that before long
you will be a very handsome dog.'

The rain had stopped by morning. The dog
went timidly into the garden, ate his breakfast
and settled down on his blanket.

'I won't be long,' Emma told him, and went
into the town to buy the local paper. There
weren't many jobs going, and the two she went
after had already been taken. She went home
dispirited, to be instantly cheered by the dog's
delight at seeing her again.

'Something will turn up,' she told him,
watching him eat a splendid dinner. 'You'll
bring me luck. You must have a name...' She
considered that for a minute or two. 'Percy,' she
told him.

She took him for a short walk later, trotting
beside her on his lead, but he was quickly tired
so she picked him up and carried him home.

And it seemed as though he *was* bringing her
luck for there were two jobs in the newsagent's
window the next day. She wrote down their ad-
dresses and went home to write to them. She
wasn't sure what a 'general assistant' in one of
the hotel's kitchens might mean, but the hotel
would be open all winter. And the second job

was part-time at an antiques shop at the end of an alley leading off Main Street. She was tempted to call there instead of writing, but that might lessen her chances of getting the job.

She posted her letters, saw to Percy's needs, had her supper and went to bed, confident that the morning would bring good news.

It brought another letter from her mother, a lengthy one, and Emma wondered at her Mother's opening words. 'At last you will be free to live your own life, Emma.'

Emma put down her teacup and started to read and when she had read it, she read it again. Her mother and her old schoolfriend had come to a decision; they would share life together.

We shall live at the cottage, but since she has a car we can go to Richmond, where she will keep her flat, whenever we want a change. I'm sure you will agree with me that this is an excellent idea, and since I shall be providing a home for her she will pay all expenses. So, Emma, you will be free to do whatever you like. Of course we shall love to see you as often as you like to come. Such a pity that there are only two bedrooms, but

*when we go to Richmond you can use the
cottage.*

Emma drank her cooling tea. She had no job,
she had received her very last pay from Miss
Johnson, and now, it seemed, she was to have
no home.

'Well, things can't get worse,' said Emma,
and offered the toast which she no longer
wanted to Percy. 'So things will get better. I'll
advertise in the paper for a live-in job where
dogs are welcome.'

Brave words! But Emma was sensible and
practical as well. There was work for anyone
who wanted it; it was just a question of finding
it. Since her mother now didn't intend to return
for another week or so she had all the time in
the world to go looking for it.

There were no replies to her two letters, but
there was still time for their answers. She didn't
give up her search, though, and filled in her
days with turning Percy into a well-groomed,
well-fed dog. He would never be handsome, and
the scar over his eye had left a bald patch, but
she considered that he was a credit to her. More
than that, he helped her to get through the disappointing days.

She had written to her mother, and it had
been a difficult letter to write. That her mother

had had no intention of upsetting her was obvious, but circumstances had arisen which would make it possible for her to live in comfort with a congenial companion and she had brushed aside any obstacles which might stand in her way. She had had no difficulty in persuading herself that Emma would be glad to be independent and she had written cheerfully to that effect, unconcerned as to how Emma would achieve that independence.

It might take a little time, Emma had pointed out, before she could find work which would pay her enough to give her her independence, but no doubt that was something which had been considered in their plans and in any case Salcombe was still full of visitors. Which wasn't quite true, but Emma had felt justified in saying so. The longer her mother delayed coming back to Salcombe the better were her chances of getting a job.

The days went by. She went to Kingsbridge by bus and spent the day searching out agencies and scanning the adverts in the newspaper shops, and finally she tried the supermarket. No chance of work, she was told roundly. They were shedding seasonal staff, and if a vacancy occurred it would go to someone local.

It was early evening by the time she got back and Percy was waiting impatiently. She fed him and took him for a walk, and went to get her own supper. Almost another week, she reflected. Unless something turns up tomorrow I shall have to write to Mother and tell her I can't leave until I can find a job...

She wasn't hungry; Percy gobbled up most of her supper and went back to sleep on his blanket and she sat down to peruse the local paper. Work was getting scarce now that the season was almost over and there was nothing there for her. She sat in the darkening evening, doing nothing—for once her cheerful optimism had left her.

Someone knocking on the door roused her and Percy gave a small squeaky bark, although he didn't get off the blanket.

Dr van Dyke was on the doorstep.

Emma was conscious of the delight and relief she felt surge through her person at the sight of him—like finding a familiar tree in a wood in which she had been lost. She stood there looking at him, saying nothing at all.

When he asked, 'May I come in?' she found her tongue.

'Yes, of course. Did you want to see me about something?'

He followed her into the living room and closed the door. He said coolly, 'No, I was walking this way and it seemed a good idea to call and see how you are getting on.' His eye fell on Percy. He lifted an eyebrow. 'Yours?'

'Yes. His name is Percy.'

He bent to stroke Percy's untidy head. 'Your mother is not home?'

'Mother's away, staying with friends in Richmond. Won't you sit down? Would you like a cup of coffee?'

She must match his coolness with her own, she thought, and sat down composedly, facing him, forgetful of the table-lamp which highlighted her face.

'What is the matter, Emma?'

The question was unexpected, and she said far too quickly, 'The matter? Why, nothing. Have you been busy at the medical centre?'

'No more than usual. I asked you what is the matter, Emma?'

He sounded kind and friendly in an impersonal way, but he watched her from under his heavy-lidded eyes. The weeks without a regular sight of her carroty topknot and their occasional brief meetings had made it plain to him that the strong attraction he felt for her had become something beyond his control; he had fallen in love with her.

He smiled at her now and she looked away quickly. 'Oh, it's nothing. I'm a bit disappointed at not finding another job, and the library doesn't want me now that summer's over...'

When he remained silent, she said with barely concealed ill-humour, 'I'll make some coffee.'

'You have no work, no money and you are lonely.'

She said waspishly, 'You've put it very clearly, and now, you know, I think you should go...'

'You will feel better if you talk to someone, and I am here, am I not? What is more, I have the added advantage of leaving Salcombe in the very near future. After all, I am a good listener; that is something which my profession has taught me—and you need a pair of ears.'

'Well, there is nothing to tell you,' said Emma rather defiantly, and burst into tears.

Dr van Dyke, by a great effort of will-power, stayed sitting in his chair. Much as he would have liked to take her into his arms, now was not the moment to show more than friendly sympathy, but presently he leaned across and stuffed his handkerchief into her hand and watched while she mopped her face, and blew her nose in an effort to return to her normal sensible manner. But her voice was a bit wobbly and she was twisting his handkerchief into a travesty of its snowy perfection.

'Well,' began Emma, and it all came tumbling out—not always in the right order, so that he had to sort out the details for himself. And when at last she had finished she muttered, 'Sorry I've made such a fool of myself. I do think it would be better if you went now; I am so ashamed of being such a cry-baby.'

Already at the back of the doctor's clever head a vague plan was taking shape. Farfetched, almost for certain to be rejected by Emma, yet it was the obvious answer. To leave her to the uncertainties of her mother's plans, workless and more or less penniless... It was something he would think over later, but for now he said cheerfully, 'I'll go if you want me to, but I think a cup of coffee would be nice first.'

She jumped up. 'Of course. I'm sorry. It won't take long.'

She went into the kitchen and laid a tray, and was putting the last few biscuits in the tin onto a plate when he followed, the dog at his heels.

'This is a charming little house. I've often admired it from the outside, and it's even nicer indoors. I like kitchens, don't you?' He glanced round him. She had left a cupboard door open and it looked empty; she was very likely not having quite enough to eat. He carried the tray back to the living room and sat for another half an hour, talking about nothing in particular, feeding a delighted Percy with some of his biscuit, taking care not to look at Emma's tear-stained face.

'Wibeke wanted to know how you were,' he told her. 'They enjoyed their holiday here. The children have all got chicken pox now; she's thankful that they're all having it at the same time.'

'They were dears, the children,' said Emma, and smiled at last. 'They must be such fun.'

'They are.' He got up to go. 'Have dinner with me tomorrow evening and we'll talk about them. Eight o'clock? Shall we see if the Gallery has any lobsters?' And when she hesitated, he added, 'I'm not asking you because I'm sorry for you, Emma, but a meal and a pleasant talk is a comfortable way to end an evening.' He glanced at Percy. 'I dare say we might be allowed to hide him under the table—the manager owes me; I stitched up his cut hand late one night.'

He didn't wait for her to answer.

As she closed the door she decided that it would be most ungracious to refuse his invitation since he had been so kind.

She went to bed and slept soundly and set off once more on her fruitless search for work in the morning, to return home to the pleasant prospect of dinner with Dr van Dyke.

Aware that she had hardly looked her best on the previous evening, she took pains with her appearance. The evenings were cool now, so she got into a dress and jacket in a soft uncrushable material. It was a subdued silvery green which made the most of her hair, which she had twisted into an old-fashioned bun at the nape of her neck. 'Out-of-date but respectable,' she told Percy, who was sitting on the bed watching her dressing.

Dr van Dyke was waiting for her, studying the board outside the restaurant. His 'Hello,' was briskly friendly. 'I see we're in luck; there's lobster on the menu.'

'Hello,' said Emma breathlessly. 'I've brought Percy—you said...'

'All arranged. Let's go in; I'm famished.'

The lobster was delicious, served simply on a bed of lettuce with a Caesar salad. They talked as they ate, unhurriedly. The place was almost empty and would close for the winter in a few days' time. Peach Melba followed, and a pot of coffee which was renewed while they talked. As for Percy, sitting silently under the table, he had a bowl of water and, quite contrary to the house rules, a plate of biscuits.

It was well after ten o'clock when they left.

Walking back to the cottage, Dr van Dyke glanced at Emma in the semi-darkness of the little quay. His plans had become reality. It was now a question of convincing Emma that they were both practical and sensible. No hint of his feelings for her must be allowed to show. This would be a businesslike arrangement with no strings attached. Now it was merely a matter of waiting for the right moment.

He unlocked the cottage door, switched on the lights, bade Percy goodnight and listened gravely to her little speech of thanks.

'It is I who thank you, Emma. Lobster is something one should never eat alone and I have much enjoyed your company.'

'I've never been compared with a lobster before,' said Emma tartly.

'I wouldn't presume to compare you with anyone or anything, Emma. Sleep soundly.'

'Oh, I will.' As he turned away she asked, 'When do you go back to Holland?'

'Very soon now. Goodnight, Emma.'

Not a very satisfactory answer.

The doctor had kindly Fate on his side; two evenings later the lifeboat was called out to go to the aid of a yacht off Prawle Point. He had just sat down to his supper when the maroon sounded and within ten minutes he was in oilskins and heavy boots, putting to sea with the rest of the crew. It was a stormy evening, will squalls of heavy rain and a strong wind. This was something he would miss, he reflected, taking up his station. When he had first come to Salcombe a crew member had fallen ill; he had volunteered to take his place and been accepted as a man who could be useful when the need arose.

Two hours later they were back in harbour, the yacht in tow, its crew led away to the Harbour Master's office for warm drinks and plans for the night. Half an hour later the doctor said goodnight and went out into the narrow lane behind the boat house. He glanced along Victoria Quay as he reached it and then lengthened his stride. Emma and Percy were just turning into the cottage gate.

She was at the door when he reached the cottage.

She saw him then, and waited at the door until he reached her, took the key from her hand, opened the door and switched on the light. She saw him clearly then: wet hair, an old pullover.

'What's happened?' she asked, and then 'You were in the lifeboat…?'

'Yes, I was on the way home when I saw you both.'

'I went up to the boat house to see if there was anything I could do. You're all safe?' When he nodded, she added, 'Would you like a hot drink? Cocoa?'

That was a drink he associated with his childhood, gulped down under Nanny's sharp eye. 'That would be most welcome. The weather's pretty rough outside the estuary.'

The little room looked cosy and smelled strongly of furniture polish. Indeed, looking round him, he could see that everything gleamed as though waiting for a special occasion, and in one corner there was a small box neatly packed with books.

Emma came back presently, with the cocoa and a tin of biscuits, and he studied her face narrowly as he got up. She looked sad, but not tearfully so, and there was a kind of quiet acceptance in her face. He had seen that look many times before on a patient's face when they had been confronted with a doubtful future.

He sipped his cocoa, pronounced it delicious, and asked, carefully casual, 'Have you heard from your mother? She plans to return soon?'

'They will be coming next week—on Wednesday.'

'And you? You have plans?'

'I'll find a job.'

'For some time now,' said the doctor casu-

ally, 'I have been badgered by my secretary in
Holland to find someone to give her a helping
hand. She does have too much to do, and when
I return there will be even more work. It has
occurred to me that perhaps you would consider
working for her? It is rather a menial job: filing
letters and running errands and dealing with
phone calls if she is engaged. She is a fierce
lady but she has a heart of gold. She speaks
English, of course. The money won't be much
but there's a room in the house where she lives
which I think you could afford.' He added, 'A
temporary measure, of course, just to tide you
over.'

'You're offering me a job in Holland?
When?'

'As from the middle of next week. Should
you consider accepting, we could leave on the
day your mother returns here, so that you could
spend some time with her. I plan to go over to
Holland on the late-night ferry from Harwich.
We wouldn't need to leave here before five
o'clock.'

'I can't,' said Emma. 'I won't leave Percy.'

'He can come with us; there's time to deal
with the formalities. Do you have a passport?
And do you drive a car?'

'Yes, to both.' She put down her mug. 'You
do mean it, don't you?'

He said evenly, 'Yes, I mean it, Emma. You would be doing Juffrouw Smit a good turn and save me hunting around for someone when I get home.'

'Where do you live?'

'Near Amsterdam. My rooms are in the city, as are the hospitals where I work. You would live in Amsterdam itself.'

He put down his mug, lifted a somnolent Percy off his knee and got up.

'It's late. Think about it and let me know in the morning.' And as she went to open the door he said again, 'The cocoa was so delicious.' He smiled down at her bewildered face. 'Sleep well.'

And strangely enough she did, and woke in the morning with her mind made up. Here was her opportunity to make a life for herself. Moreover, it meant that she would still see Dr van Dyke from time to time. He was kind and thoughtful, he liked dogs and children, and he had offered her a job...

'It's a pity that I don't appeal to him as a woman,' said Emma to Percy. 'It's my hair, of course, and bawling my eyes out all over him.'

She would have to let him know and without waste of time. But first she made sure that she had her passport, and then she sat down to tot up her money. She would leave half of it in the bank and take the rest with her; she might not be paid for a month and she would have to live until then.

It wasn't much but it would give her security, and she would arrange with the bank that her mother could use the money there. She would have to bear in mind that her mother and her friend might agree to part later on, in which case she would have to return. But there was no point in thinking about that; her mother had been quite positive about her plans and made it clear that Emma had no part in them.

The doctor's surgeries would be over by eleven o'clock; she went to the medical centre and waited until the last patient had gone and then knocked on Dr van Dyke's door. He was sitting at his desk but he got up as she went in.

'Emma—sit down.' When she did, he sat back in his chair again. 'And what have you decided?'

'When I went to bed last night,' said Emma carefully, 'I decided to make up my mind this morning—think about it before I went to sleep. Only I went to sleep first, and when I woke up this morning my mind had made itself up. If you think I could do the job you offered me, I'd like to accept.'

'Good. Now, as to details: you will work from eight o'clock in the morning until five in the afternoon. An hour and a half for lunch at noon, half an hour for tea at half past three. You must be prepared to turn your hand to anything which Juffrouw Smit or I ask of you. You will be free on Saturday and Sunday, although if the occasion should arise you might need to work on either of those two days. You will be paid weekly.' He named a sum in guilders and then changed it into English pounds. It seemed a generous amount, and when she looked questioningly at him, he said, 'It's the going rate for a job such as yours, and you will earn it. Juffrouw Smit expects the best. Do you still want to come?'

He was friendly, but he was brisk too. This was a businesslike meeting, she reminded herself. She said quietly, 'Yes, I still want to come. If you will tell me where to go and when...'

'You will go over to Holland with me. You will need your passport, of course, not too much luggage—and Percy. You will perhaps let your mother know that we will leave in the late afternoon on Wednesday, so that she can arrange to be here before you leave? You are quite sure that is what she wants?'

'Yes. She—she has never been happy living here with me, but I think she will settle down with her friend. They like the same things: bridge and driving around the country and being able to go back to Richmond when they want to. And if it doesn't turn out as they hoped, then I'll come back here...'

'Just so,' agreed the doctor. If he had a hand in it that would be the last thing his darling Emma would do.

He said smoothly, 'Shall we settle some of the details? I'll see about Percy and arrange the journey. I'll come down to the cottage at five o'clock on Wednesday. It will be quite a long drive and we shan't get to Amsterdam until well after midnight. Will you have much luggage?'

'A case and a shoulder bag.'

Going home presently, she thought how coolly businesslike he had been. Since he was to be her employer, perhaps that was a good thing. She took Percy for a brisk walk and set about the task of sorting out her clothes. She wouldn't need much; she doubted if she would have much social life...

Her tweed jacket and skirt, the cashmere twin-set, a grey jersey dress which she thought might do for her work, another skirt—jersey again because it could be squeezed into a corner without creasing—blouses and a thin sweater, and, as a concession to the social life she didn't expect, a sapphire-blue dress which could be folded into almost nothing and remained band-box-fresh. 'Shoes,' said Emma to a watchful Percy. 'And I'll wear my winter coat and cram in a raincoat, gloves, handbag, undies and dressing gown...'

She laid everything out on the bed in her mother's bedroom and, being a sensible girl, sat down and wrote out all the things she had to do before Wednesday.

There was a letter from her mother in the morning. She and Mrs Riddley would arrive during the morning on Wednesday.

We shall spend the night on the way, and get to you in good time for coffee. Just a light lunch will do because we shall eat out in the evening. I expect you have arranged everything; I'm sure that by now you must have found just the kind of job you would like. Far be it from me to stand in the way of your ambition...

Emma put down the letter. She loved her mother, and she hoped that her mother loved her, but that lady had a way of twisting circumstances to suit herself, ignoring the fact that those same circumstances might not suit anyone else. Emma had known that since she was a small girl and had accepted it; her mother had

been a very pretty woman, and charming, and
Emma had grown up taking it for granted that
she must be shielded from worry or unpleas-
antness. There had been little of either until her
father had died, and she didn't blame her
mother for wishing her former carefree life to
continue.

She went the next day to say goodbye to Miss
Johnson and Phoebe. Miss Johnson wished her
well and told her to be sure and visit the splendid museums in Amsterdam, and Phoebe looked
at her with envy.

'Lucky you, going to work for Dr van Dyke.
What wouldn't I give to be in your shoes?
Going for keeps or coming back here later?'

'I'm not going for keeps,' said Emma, 'and
I dare say I'll come back later on.'

She met Mrs Craig the next day.

'My dear Emma, the very person I want to
see. I had a card from your mother. How excited
you must be. It's good news that she is going
to stay in Salcombe—bringing a friend with her,
she tells me.' She gave a little laugh. 'The cottage is rather small for three of you…'

'I won't be here,' said Emma. 'I'm going to
work for Dr van Dyke when he goes back to
Amsterdam. At least, I shall be working with
his secretary. I'm to have lodgings with her.
I've been working at the medical centre and I

liked the work. It would have been difficult fitting three of us into the cottage, as you say.'

'Your mother will miss you.'

'Her friend is delighted to take my place—they have known each other since schooldays. She's very much looking forward to being here and meeting you and Mother's other friends.'

Mrs Craig studied Emma's face. There was no sign of worry or annoyance on it, all the same she didn't sound quite right.

Emma bade her a cheerful goodbye and hurried home to take Percy for his walk. He was becoming quite handsome, with a gleaming coat, melting brown eyes and a long feathery tail. Only his ears were on the large side, and she suspected that he wasn't going to grow much larger. She had told him that he was going to live in another country with her and he had wagged his tail in a pleased fashion. This was only to be expected, considering the doubtful life he had been leading in Salcombe.

Her mother and Mrs Riddley arrived in a flurry of greetings and embracing and gentle grumbling because they'd had to leave the car by the pub and there was no one to carry their luggage.

'Do find someone, darling,' said Mrs Dawson plaintively. 'And I quite forgot to ask you to find someone to clean the place for us.'

Emma accepted the car keys. 'Well, it's a bit late for me to do anything about that now,' she said cheerfully, 'but there are plenty of adverts in the newsagent's. I'll see what I can do about your luggage. Don't let Percy out of the gate, will you?'

'Such an ugly little dog,' said Mrs Riddley. 'But of course you'll take him with you?'

'Yes,' said Emma. 'We shall be gone this afternoon.'

She didn't like Mrs Riddley. Emma had heard of her from her mother from time to time but they had never met, though she could quite see that she would be an ideal companion for her mother. Another one skimming over the surface of life, making light of anything serious or unpleasant, being fashionable and excellent company; her mother would be happy with her.

The odd-job man at the pub helped with the luggage and Emma lugged it upstairs. She left the two ladies to begin their unpacking while she got the lunch, and over that meal she listened to their plans and intentions.

'We two old ladies intend to keep each other company while you go off and enjoy yourself. You're only young once, Emma. How wise of you to decide to see something of the world.'

Just as though I had planned the whole thing, reflected Emma. She felt bitterly hurt at her mother's bland acceptance of her leaving home, and felt as guilty as though she had actually arranged the whole thing herself. But there was no doubt that her mother was happy; she had convinced herself that Emma was pleasing herself, and beyond saying that it was so fortunate that Emma was going to work for someone she already knew she didn't want to know about the job itself.

After lunch Mrs Dawson said, 'You must tell me what you have done about the bank account. Dear Alice will see to the bills, since she is living here rent-free, but I must contribute towards the housekeeping, I suppose, and that will leave me almost penniless.'

'There's an account in your name at the bank. I've put in all the money I've earned except for the last two weeks' wages. I don't know what expenses I'll have until I've been in Amsterdam for a while and I won't get paid until the end of the month.'

'A good salary? You'll be able to help me out if I get short, darling?'

'Don't depend on that, mother. I shan't be earning much and I'll have to pay for food and lodgings.'

Her mother pouted. 'Oh, well, I suppose I'll just have to manage as best I can. Your father would turn in his grave, Emma...'

Emma didn't speak because she was swallowing tears. But presently she said, 'I must take Percy for a walk. I'll prepare tea when I come back.'

She took quite a long walk: round the end of Victoria Quay and round the back of the town and back through the main street. She wasn't sure when she would see it again, with its small shops and the friendly people in them. She waved to the butcher as she went past, and even the cross-faced woman at the bakery smiled.

They had finished their tea and Emma had washed up and put everything ready for the morning when Dr van Dyke came.

She introduced him, and she could see that the two ladies were impressed. He looked—she sought for words—respectable, and he said all the right things. But he didn't waste time; he told her that they must leave and made his goodbyes with the beautiful manners which her mother and Mrs Riddley obviously admired.

And then it was her turn to make her farewells, sent on her way with cheerful hopes that she would have a lovely time and to be sure and send a card when she had time. 'And don't forget your poor old mother,' said Mrs Dawson in a wispier voice than usual—which sent Emma out of the door feeling that she was an uncaring daughter deserting her mother.

She walked beside the doctor, with Percy on his lead, and he took her case and shoulder bag. He didn't look at her, and it wasn't until she was in the car beside him that she muttered, 'I feel an absolute heel...'

He still didn't look at her. 'Your mother is a charming lady, Emma, but you mustn't believe all she says. She was merely uttering a remark which she felt suited the occasion. She will be very happy with her friend—I believe that and so must you—far happier than living with you; you must see that for yourself. You may love each other dearly but you are as unlike as chalk from cheese.'

Emma sniffed; she had no intention of crying although she felt like it.

His large comforting hand covered hers for a moment. 'You must believe me; she will be happy and so will you.'

CHAPTER FIVE

EMMA sat beside the doctor, watching the quiet Devon countryside flash past as he made for the A38 and Exeter. He had told her that everything would be all right and she had to believe him, although she was beset by doubts. Juffrouw Smit might dislike her on sight; she might not be able to cope with the work. She would have to acquire at least a smattering of Dutch—and would she be able to live on her wages?

And over and above all that there was the unhappy thought that somehow or other she must make a success of the job, stay there until she had experience and some money saved before she could return to England. And what then? Her mother would be glad to see her as long as she didn't upset her life. Perhaps she would never be able to go back to the cottage at Salcombe...

'Stop worrying,' said Dr van Dyke. 'Take each day as it comes, and when you have found your feet you can make your plans. And I promise you that if you are unhappy in Amsterdam then I will see that you get back to England.'

'You're very kind,' said Emma. 'It's silly of me to fuss, and actually I'm rather looking forward to working for your Juffrouw Smit.'

He began to talk then, a gentle meandering conversation which required few answers on her part but which somehow soothed her. By the time they had bypassed Exeter, left the A30 and joined the A303, she actually felt quite light-hearted.

At the doctor's speed it didn't take long to reach the M25 and take the road to Harwich, but first they stopped at Fleet, parked the car, took Percy for a run and went to the café for coffee and sandwiches.

'We can get something else on board,' said the doctor, 'and of course there will be someone waiting for us when we get home.'

'In Amsterdam? Not at Juffrouw Smit's house?'

'No, no, I wouldn't dare to disturb her night's sleep. I live a few miles outside the city. You'll spend the night at my house and go to Juffrouw Smit in the morning.' He glanced at his watch and sent the great car surging forward. 'We are almost at Harwich. You're not tired?'

'No. I've enjoyed the trip; it's a lovely car.' She peered over her shoulder. 'Percy's asleep.'

They were very nearly the last on board the ferry. The doctor drove on, tucked Percy under one arm and ushered Emma to a seat.

'Make yourself comfortable. It's a short crossing—about three and a half hours. It may be a bit choppy but it is most convenient with the car, and the catamaran is as steady as an ordinary ferry.'

'I'm not nervous.'

'Coffee and a brandy, I think, and something to eat. I'll order while you trot off...'

How nicely put, thought Emma, making a beeline for the ladies'.

They ate their sandwiches, drank their coffee and brandy, and presently the doctor got some papers out of his briefcase. 'You don't mind if I do some work?'

She shook her head, nicely drowsy from the brandy, and, with her arms wrapped round a sleeping Percy, presently she slept too.

The doctor's hand on her arm woke her. 'We're about to dock. Better give me Percy.'

It was dark and chilly and she could see very little of her surroundings.

'Not long now,' said Dr van Dyke, and swept the car onto a lighted highway. After a few minutes there were no houses, just the road ahead of them, and Emma closed her eyes again.

When she woke she could see the lights of Amsterdam, but before they reached the outskirts the doctor took an exit road and plunged into the darkness of the countryside. But not for long, for there were a few trees, and then a house or two, and then a village—nice old houses lining the narrow road. She glimpsed a church—closed now, of course—and a tall iron railing, before he turned the car between brick pillars, along a short straight drive and stopped before the house.

'You had better go straight to bed. I'll see to Percy.' He got out of the car, lifted Percy off the back seat, opened her door and urged her out.

She stood a minute, looking around her, for a moment wide awake. The house was large and square, with white walls and a steep gabled roof. The massive door was open and there were lights in some of the windows.

'Is this your home?' asked Emma.

'Yes.' He sounded impatient, so she trod up the steps to the door beside him and went into the hall. It was large and square, with doors on all sides and a vast expanse of black and white tiled floor. There was a rather grand staircase curving up one wall, and a chandelier which cast brilliant light over everything. She saw all that in one rapid glance before the doctor at her elbow said, 'This is my housekeeper, Mevrouw Kulk—Katje, this is Miss Emma Dawson.' And when they had shaken hands, he spoke to Katje in Dutch.

Mevrouw Kulk was tall, stout and dignified, but she had a cheerful smiling face. She was answering the doctor when a door at the back of the hall opened and a middle-aged man came towards them.

He went to the doctor and shook hands, saying something in an apologetic voice. The doctor laughed and turned to Emma. 'This is Kulk. He and his wife run my home. He is apologising because he wasn't here to greet us. He was shutting my dog into the kitchen.'

Emma shook hands and looked anxiously at Percy, standing obediently by the doctor's feet. 'Shall I take him with me? He'll only need a minute or two outside...'

'Go with Mevrouw Kulk. She will show you your room, bring you a hot drink and see you safely into bed. I'll see to Percy and she will bring him up when you're in bed. He'd better be with you tonight.'

Mevrouw Kulk smiled and nodded and beckoned, and the doctor said briskly, 'Sleep well, Emma. Breakfast at half past eight, before I take you to Juffrouw Smit.'

Emma followed the housekeeper upstairs.

I'm twenty-seven, she thought sleepily, and he's ordering me around as though I were a child. But she was too tired to bother about that.

The stairs opened onto a gallery with doors on every side. Mevrouw Kulk opened one and ushered Emma inside.

Emma had an instant impression of warmth and light. The mahogany bed had a soft pink quilt, matching the curtains at the window. There was a small table, with a triple mirror on it and a slender-legged stool before it, and on either side of the bed there was a small table bearing pink-shaded lamps. A lovely room, but surely not one in which Percy would be allowed to sleep?

The housekeeper turned down the coverlet. 'Bed,' she said firmly, and smiled and nodded and went away.

Emma kicked off her shoes and dug her feet into the soft white carpet. Someone had already brought her luggage to her room. She found a nightie and, since it seemed the only thing to do, had a quick shower in the small, splendidly equipped bathroom next door. She got into bed just in time; Mevrouw Kulk was back again, this time with Percy prancing beside her and a blanket over one arm, which she spread at the end of the bed. She nodded and smiled once more, to return within a minute with a small tray, containing hot milk and a plate of biscuits.

'Dr van Dyke says, "Eat, drink and sleep!"'

She patted Emma's shoulder in a motherly fashion and went away again.

So Emma drank the milk, shared the biscuits with Percy, put her head on the pillow and slept—to be wakened in the morning by a buxom girl with a tea tray. There was a note on the tray: *Let Percy go with Anneke; she can take him for a run in the garden.*

Breakfast was at half past eight and it was already eight o'clock. She showered and dressed, wishing she had more time to take pains with her face and hair, and went downstairs, wondering where she should go.

Kulk was in the hall. His 'Good morning, Miss', was uttered in a fatherly fashion as he opened a door and invited her to go past him into the room beyond. This was a small room with a bright fire burning in the steel fireplace, its windows open onto the gardens beyond. There was a round table set for breakfast, a scattering of comfortable chairs, bookshelves overflowing with books, and small tables just where they were needed. The walls were panelled and the ceiling was a magnificent example of strap work.

Emma rotated slowly as the doctor came in

from the garden. There was a mastiff beside him and, trotting as close as he could get, Percy.

His good morning was brisk. 'Percy and Prince are the best of friends, as you can see. You slept well? Shall we have breakfast?'

Emma had bent to stroke Percy. 'What a beautiful dog you have.' She held out a fist and Prince came close and breathed gently over it, then went back to stand by his master. Kulk came in then, with a loaded tray, and the doctor sent the dogs outside into the garden while they ate.

Emma was hungry. It seemed a long time since she had sat down to a decent meal, and as if he had read her thoughts Dr van Dyke observed, 'I do apologise for depriving you of a meal yesterday. You must allow me to make up for that once you have settled in.'

An invitation to dinner, thought Emma, loading marmalade onto toast. What a good thing I brought that dress. But all she said was, 'That would be very nice,' in a non-committal voice. It might be one of those half-meant, vague invitations exchanged so often amongst friends and acquaintances when she lived in Richmond, which never materialised. But no one had expected them to anyway.

Given no more than a few minutes in which to collect her things and thank the Kulks for their kindness, she was urged into the car, her luggage put in the boot, and Percy, waiting on the doorstep, was put on the back seat. Since the doctor had nothing to say, she held her tongue. She knew him well enough by now to understand that if there was nothing she should know she should be quiet.

Amsterdam was surprisingly close: first the modern outskirts and then the real Amsterdam—narrow streets and gabled houses leaning against each other lining the canals.

The doctor stopped before a row of old red-brick houses with imposing fronts.

'I shall be a few minutes,' he told her, before he got out and went inside one of the houses, which gave her time to look around her. There were several brass plates beside the door; this would be his consulting rooms, then. Very stylish, thought Emma.

He got back into the car presently. 'My consulting rooms,' he told her. 'You will work here with Juffrouw Smit.'

He swung the car down a narrow lane with small houses on either side of it and stopped again before one of them. He helped her out, scooped up Percy and rang the old-fashioned bell. The door was opened immediately by a lady who could have been a close relation of Miss Johnson: the same stiff hairstyle, white blouse and cardigan and sensible skirt, the same severe expression. Emma felt a surge of relief; it was like meeting an old friend...

'Good morning, Doctor, and I presume, Miss Dawson?' Her eyes fastened on Percy. 'And the little dog. Come in. Will you have coffee? You have an appointment at ten o'clock, Doctor...'

'How nice to see you again, Smitty. I must go to the hospital first, so I had better get along. Bring Emma round with you, will you? Give her some idea of her work. She can settle in this afternoon.' He smiled down at Emma. 'Juffrouw Smit, this is Emma Dawson. I'm sure she will be an apt pupil.' And when the two women had shaken hands, he said, 'I'll be off.'

Juffrouw Smit shut the door behind his vast back. 'Coffee first, then a quick look at your room before we go round to the doctor's rooms. We will speak English, but once you have found your feet you must learn a little Dutch.'

She led the way out of the tiny hall into a small sitting room, rather too full of old-fashioned furniture but very cosy. 'Sit down. I'll fetch the coffee.'

When it was poured Emma said, 'Did you know that I had Percy?'

'Yes, Dr van Dyke told me. I have a small garden with a very high wall and I shall leave the kitchen door open for him. He will be alone,

but not for long, for I come home for my meals
and if there are no patients you can slip back
for a few minutes. He will be happy?'

'He was a stray, and I've had to leave him
alone from time to time, but I'm sure he'll be
happy. You don't mind?'

'Not at all. Drink your coffee, then come and
see your room. The doctor took your luggage
up before he went.'

It was a small low-ceilinged room, overlooking the lane, very clean and cheerful, with simple furniture and a bed against one wall.

'My room is at the back of the house and
there is a bathroom between. And if you should
wish to be alone there is a small room beside
the kitchen.'

Emma looked out of the window, trying to
find a suitable way of asking about the rent;
Juffrouw Smit wasn't like the usual landlady.

It was her companion who said briskly, 'Dr
van Dyke is paying me for your room and
board; that is why your wages are small.'

'Oh, thank you. Your English is so perfect,
Juffrouw Smit—have you lived in England?'

'For several years some time ago. You will
find that most people here speak English, although we appreciate foreigners speaking our
language.'

Of course I'm a foreigner, reflected Emma, although I don't feel like one.

They settled Percy on a blanket in the kitchen, with the door open into the neat garden, and walked to the doctor's rooms. Two or three minutes brought them to the imposing door and across the equally imposing hall to another door with his name on it. Juffrouw Smit had a key and led the way into a short hallway which opened into a well-furnished waiting room—comfortable chairs, small tables with magazines, bowls of flowers and a desk in one corner.

'Through here,' said Juffrouw Smit, and opened the door by the desk. 'This is where we keep patients' notes, the account book, business letters and so on.' She shut the door, swept Emma across the room and opened another door. 'Dr van Dyke's consulting room. The door over there leads to the examination room.'

She led the way out again. 'This last door is where we make tea and coffee, and here is a cloakroom.'

Emma took it all in, rather overwhelmed. She had never thought of the doctor as being well-known and obviously wealthy. She thought of the understated luxury of his consulting room and remembered his rather bare little room at the medical centre in Salcombe. His lovely

house, too. He had never given her an inkling—
but then, why should he? She had come over
here to work and as such would hardly be expected to take a deep interest in his personal
life. He had, of course, got one; she wished she
knew more about it.

'Sit here, by my desk,' said Juffrouw Smit,
'and watch carefully. You must learn the routine before you will be any use to me.'

Emma, obediently making herself unobtru-
sive, reflected that Juffrouw Smit was every bit
as severe as Miss Johnson.

The first person to arrive was Dr van Dyke,
crossing to his own room with a brief nod, and
five minutes later an imposing matron who replied graciously to Juffrouw Smit's greeting and
ignored Emma. She was followed at suitable in-
tervals by a fat man with a red face, a thin lady
looking frightened, and lastly a sulky teenager
with a fierce-looking parent.

When they had gone, Juffrouw Smit said,
'This is a typical morning. Dr van Dyke goes
next to one or other of the hospitals where he
is a consultant, and returns here around mid-
afternoon, when he will see more patients. Very
occasionally he sees patients in the evening.
Now, if you will make the coffee and take him
a cup, we will have ours and I will explain your
work to you.'

'Do I knock?' asked Emma, cup and saucer in hand.

'Yes, and no need to speak unless he does.'

She knocked and went in. He was sitting at his desk, writing, and he didn't look up. She put the coffee on his desk and went out again, vaguely disappointed. He could at least have lifted his head and smiled...

She and Juffrouw Smit had their coffee and she took the cups back to the little cubbyhole. When she got back it was to see the doctor's back disappearing through the door.

'Now,' said Juffrouw Smit, 'listen carefully...'

Her tasks were simple: fetching and carrying, making coffee, answering the phone if Juffrouw Smit was unable to do so with the quickly learned words *'een ogenblik'*, which it seemed was a polite way of saying 'hold on'. She must see that the doctor's desk was exactly as he liked it each morning, tidy the newspapers and magazines, and, once she felt at ease with these jobs, she was expected to find and file away patients' notes and sort the post.

'Many small tasks,' observed Juffrouw Smit, 'of which I shall be relieved so that I can attend to the administration—the paperwork.'

They went back to her house for their lunch, and then Emma took Percy for a quick run before they went back to the consulting rooms and another afternoon of patients. The doctor, coming and going, did no more than nod as he went, with a brief, 'Settling in?' not waiting for an answer.

Quite a nice day, thought Emma, curling up in bed that night. Under Juffrouw Smit's severe exterior, she felt sure lurked a nice middle-aged lady who would one day become a friend. And the work, so far, wasn't beyond her. She had a pleasant room, and enough to eat, and Percy had been made welcome. The niggardly thought that the doctor seemed to have forgotten all about her she dismissed. Any fanciful ideas in that direction were to be eschewed at once...

The next day went well, despite the fact that the patients seemed endless. Excepting for a brief lunch there was no respite, so that when the last patient had gone, soon after five o'clock, and Juffrouw Smit told her to get her coat and go to the post office with a pile of letters, she was glad to do so.

It was an early dusk, and chilly, but it was lovely to be out of doors after the warmth of the waiting room. The post office was five minutes' walk away; Emma went over the little bridge at the end of the street, turned left and followed the canal. The post office was on the corner, facing a busy main road thick with traf-

fic, trams and people. She would have liked to
have lingered, taken a quick look around, but
that would have to wait until she was free tomorrow. She hurried back and found Juffrouw
Smit still at her desk, with no sign of the doctor.

'Take the key,' said Juffrouw Smit, 'and go
to my house. Perhaps you would put everything
ready for our meal? *Zuurkool* and potatoes and
a smoked sausage. Put them all on a very low
gas and feed Percy. I shall be another ten
minutes. While I cook our meal you can take
him for his walk.'

So Emma went back to the little house, to be
greeted by a delighted Percy and deal with the
saucepans and wait for Juffrouw Smit.

Juffrouw Smit was sitting opposite the doctor's
desk, listening to him.

'Yes,' she told him, 'Miss Dawson—who
wishes to be called Emma—has settled in without fuss. A sensible girl with nice manners, and
quick to grasp what is wanted of her.' Juffrouw
Smit fixed the doctor with a sharp eye. 'Do you
wish me to train her to take my place, doctor?'

'Take your place? Smitty, you surely don't
want to retire? There are years ahead of you.
You surely never supposed that that was in my
mind? I cannot imagine being without you. No,
no, I will explain...'

Which he did, though giving away none of his true feelings, but as Juffrouw Smit got up to go and reached the door she turned to look at him.

'You wish to marry Emma, Doctor?'

He glanced up from the papers he was turning over. 'That is my intention, Smitty.'

The smile he gave her warmed her spinster's heart.

Emma, unaware of the future planned for her, took Percy for a brisk walk, noting the names of the streets as she went. The ranks of tall old houses all looked rather alike, and so did the canals. As she went back she passed the consulting rooms and saw the lights were still on. She hoped the doctor wasn't sitting there working when he should be at home with that magnificent dog. Kulk should be offering him a stiff drink after his day's work while Mevrouw Kulk cooked him a delicious meal. It would be nice to see the house again, but she doubted if she would.

That evening she listened to Juffrouw Smit's suggestions—clearly to be taken most seriously—concerning her washing and ironing, the time of the day when she might consider the bathroom to be hers, and the household chores she was expected to do—which weren't many, for a stout woman came twice each week to clean. Emma must keep her room clean and tidy, and help with the cooking and tidying of the kitchen.

Armed with a Dutch dictionary, and a phrase-book Juffrouw Smit gave her, Emma spent a good deal of her evening in the small room beside the kitchen. Only just before bedtime did she join Juffrouw Smit in the sitting room for a last cup of coffee before saying goodnight. They talked a little then, and watched the news, before she let Percy into the garden prior to taking him upstairs with her.

For the moment Emma was content; it was all new to her and it would be several weeks before she would feel anything other than a lodger. A day out tomorrow—Saturday—she decided. She would get a map of the city and find her way around at her leisure, and on Sunday she would go to church—there would surely be an English Church? And she would write letters in the little room, out of Juffrouw Smit's way.

She had written home once already, a brief letter telling her mother of her safe arrival, with the address and phone number. She would buy postcards too, and send them to Phoebe and Miss Johnson and Mrs Craig. And find a book-shop...

She went to bed with a head full of cheerful plans. Juffrouw Smit had listened to them and nodded and offered a street map, and told her where she would find the English church. She had observed that she herself would be spending Saturday with a cousin and on Sunday would be going to her own church in the morning.

'So you must feel free to spend your days as you wish, Emma. You have a key, and I hope you will do as you wish and treat my house as your home.'

Emma told herself that she was a very lucky girl; she had a job, a home, and Percy—and, as well as that, her mother was once more happy.

She helped to wash up and tidy the little house in the morning and then went to her room to get her jacket and her handbag. When she went downstairs Percy was in the hall waiting for her. So were Juffrouw Smit and Dr van Dyke.

His good morning was genial. 'If you feel like a walk I thought I might show you some of Amsterdam. It can be a little confusing to a stranger...'

She stared up at him. 'Thank you, but I wouldn't dream of wasting your time. I have a street map...'

'Oh, but I'm much easier to understand than

a street map.' He smiled at her. 'The canals can be very confusing, don't you agree, Smitty?'

'Oh, undoubtedly, Doctor. And it will be much quicker for Emma to find her way around once she has been guided by someone who knows the city.' She said briskly to Emma, 'You have your key?'

Emma nodded, trying to think of something to say which wouldn't sound rude; she was having her day arranged for her, and although it would be delightful to spend it with the doctor she couldn't help but feel that he was performing a charitable act prompted by good manners. To refuse wasn't possible; rudeness was something she had been brought up to avoid at all costs, so she said quietly, 'You're very kind. May I bring Percy?'

'Of course. He'll be company for Prince.'

They bade Juffrouw Smit goodbye and went out into the street. The Rolls was there, with Prince in the driver's seat, and Emma came to a halt.

'I was going to explore Amsterdam...'

'So we will, but first we will go back to my place and have coffee, and leave Prince and Percy in Kulk's charge; neither of them would enjoy sightseeing, you know.'

This statement was uttered in such a reasonable voice that there was no answer...besides, it was obvious when they reached his house that Percy was delighted to be handed over to the care of Kulk and Prince's fatherly company.

She was ushered into the room where they had had breakfast and the dogs rushed out into the garden as Kulk came in with the coffee tray. Emma, pouring coffee from the silver pot into paper-thin cups, allowed herself to enjoy the quiet luxury of the doctor's household. A pity, she thought as she nibbled a wafer-thin biscuit, that she couldn't see behind the ornate double doors on the other side of the hall. It was a large house, and doubtless full of lovely furniture...

She made polite small talk, encouraged by the doctor's grave replies, but it was a relief when he suggested that she might like to tidy herself before they went back to Amsterdam.

He parked the Rolls outside his consulting rooms. 'I shall show you the lay-out of the city,' he told her, 'so that you are familiar with the main streets. We shall walk first to the station. Think of it as the centre of a spider's web. The main streets radiate from it and the canals encircle it. Always carry Juffrouw Smit's address with you, and my telephone number, and keep to the main streets until you know your way around.'

He walked her briskly to the station, then down Damrak to Damrak Square, where he allowed her a moment to view the royal palace and the memorial before taking her through Kalverstraat, lined with shops, to the Leidesgracht, into the Herengracht and into Vizelstraat back towards the Dam Square.

He took her to lunch then, in a large hotel close to the flower market and the Mint, and Emma, her appetite sharpened by their lengthy walking, ate smoked eel—which she hadn't expected to like but which turned out to be simply delicious—followed by sole *meunière* with a salad and a dessert of profiteroles and whipped cream. Pouring coffee, she said in her sensible way, 'That was a lovely lunch. Thank you!'

'Good. Now I will show you where the museums are, and the churches, the Town Hall, the hospitals and the post office and banks.'

So off they went once more. It was hardly a social outing, reflected Emma, conscious that her feet were beginning to ache, excepting for the lunch, of course. On the other hand it was going to make finding her way around the city much easier.

It was four o'clock when he said finally, 'You would like a cup of tea,' and ushered her to a small elegant café. She sank into a chair and eased her feet out of her shoes, drank the tea and ate a mountainous pastry swimming in cream and then pushed her feet back into her shoes once again.

It was a relief to find that they were only a short walk from Juffrouw Smit's house, and when they were in sight of it the doctor said, 'I've tired you out. Go indoors; I'll fetch Percy.'

If her feet hadn't been hurting so much perhaps she might have demurred. As it was she went thankfully into the house and he went at once. 'Fifteen minutes,' he told her, and was gone.

She had her shoes off and her slippers on, her outdoor things put away and everything ready for coffee by the time he returned with Percy.

She opened the door to him, embraced Percy and politely offered coffee.

The doctor stood looking at her. The bright overhead light in the little hall had turned her fiery head into a rich glow, and the long walk had given her a splendid colour. The temptation to gather her into his arms and kiss her was great, but he resisted it, well aware that this wasn't the time or the place.

'Would you like coffee?' asked Emma.

'I've an appointment,' he told her. 'I do hope I haven't tired you too much?'

'No, no. I've enjoyed every minute of it—and it will be so helpful now that I've a good idea of the city. It was a lovely day. Thank you very much.'

He smiled, then bade her goodbye and went away.

It seemed very quiet in the little house when he had gone. She made dark coffee, fed Percy and thought about her day. Being with the doctor had been delightful, for he was a good companion and she felt quite at ease in his company, but she doubted if there would be many occasions such as today. He had felt it his duty, no doubt, to make her familiar with Amsterdam, since she had had no chance to do anything about it herself, and probably he felt responsible about her since she was in his employ. And that was something she must never forget, for all his friendliness.

Juffrouw Smit had said that she would be late home, so Emma got her own supper presently, and wrote a letter to her mother. She had plenty to write about, and she had only just finished it when Juffrouw Smit came back. They sat together for an hour over coffee, exchanging news of their day until bedtime.

Tomorrow, thought Emma sleepily, curling up in her bed, I shall go to church, have lunch somewhere and explore. The quicker she felt at home in Amsterdam the better.

She found the little church in the Beguine

Court, which the doctor had told her about, and after the service wandered around looking at the charming little houses surrounding it before going in search of a small café.

Much refreshed by a *kaas broodje* and coffee, she found her way to the station, bought a timetable with an eye to future expeditions, and then boarded a sightseeing boat to tour the canals.

The boat was full, mostly with Americans and English, and the guide kept up a running commentary as they went from one canal to the other. It gave her a splendid back-to-front view of the city, with the lovely old houses backing onto the canals, some with high-walled gardens, some of their windows almost at water level. If she had had the time she would have gone round again for a second time, but it was almost four o'clock and she intended to have tea before she went back to Juffrouw Smit.

She found the café where the doctor had taken her, and, reckless of the prices, had tea and an enormous confection of cream and meringue and chocolate. Then, well satisfied with her day, she went back to Juffrouw Smit's little house.

They spent a pleasant evening together, talking about nothing much while Juffrouw Smit knitted a complicated pattern with enviable ease. Beyond hoping that she had enjoyed her day she asked no questions as to what Emma had done with it, nor did she vouchsafe any information as to her own day. Emma sensed that although they liked each other they would never become friendly enough to exchange personal feelings. But it was enough that they could live together in harmony.

The days went smoothly enough. As the week progressed Emma found herself taking on more and more of the trivial jobs at the consulting rooms, so that Juffrouw Smit could spend more time at her desk, dealing with the computer, the e-mails and the fax machine. For all her staid appearance, there was nothing lacking in her modern skills.

These were things Emma supposed she would have to master if she wished to make a career for herself, but first she supposed that she must learn at least a smattering of the Dutch language. She must ask Juffrouw Smit if there were evening classes. But for the moment it was enough that she had a roof over her head, a job and her wages.

Towards the end of the week she had a letter from her mother. Mrs Dawson was happy—something she had never been with her, thought Emma wistfully, but it was good to know that she was finding life fun again. She and Alice, she wrote, had settled in well. They had found a woman to look after the place, and they had joined a bridge club. They had coffee with Mrs Craig and various friends each morning, and the boutique had such lovely clothes for the winter. At the end of the letter Mrs Dawson hoped that Emma had settled in happily and was getting to know some young people and having fun. *You really must learn to enjoy life more, darling!* She didn't ask about Emma's work.

Emma, stifling hurt feelings, was glad that her mother was once again living the kind of life she had always enjoyed. She wrote back cheerfully.

Otherwise she spent her evenings poring over the Dutch dictionary, and replied with a cool politeness to the doctor's brief greetings as he came and went each day.

She had been there almost a month when she decided that she could afford to buy a winter coat. She had learned her way around Amsterdam by now, and there were side streets where there were little dress shops where one might pick up a bargain...

Her pay packet crackling nicely in her pocket, she was getting out the case sheets for the day's patients when the doctor came out of his room. He put a letter on the desk and turned to go back.

'Please see that your letters are addressed to

Juffrouw Smit's house and not to my rooms,'
he observed pleasantly, and had gone again before Emma could utter an apology.

She picked up the letter. It looked official,
typewritten and sent by the overnight express
mail. She opened it slowly—had she left an un-
paid bill? Or was it something to do with the
bank?

She began to read.

CHAPTER SIX

IT WAS from Mr Trump. This would be a severe shock to her, he wrote, but her mother and her friend Mrs Riddley had died instantly in a car crash while making a short visit to friends at Richmond. Fortunately, someone who knew them had phoned him at once and he was dealing with the tragic matter. He had not known how to reach her on the phone but begged her to ring him as soon as possible. It was a kind letter and he assured her of his support and assistance.

She read it through again, standing in the cubbyhole, until Juffrouw Smit's voice, a little impatient, penetrated the blankness of her mind. Would she take the doctor's coffee in at once, or he would have no time to drink it before the first patient arrived.

She made the coffee, filled his cup and carried cup and saucer across to his door, knocked and went in. As she set them down on his desk he looked up, saw her ashen face and promptly got up to take her in his arms.

'Emma, what's wrong? Are you ill?' He remembered the letter. 'Bad news?'

She didn't trust herself to speak but fished the letter out of her pocket. Still with one arm round her, he read it.

'My poor dear girl. What shocking news.' He sat her down in the chair facing his desk and pressed the button which would light the discreet red light on Juffrouw Smit's desk. When that lady came, he said, 'Smitty, Emma has had bad news from England. Will you bring her some brandy, then delay my first patient if she comes on time?'

When she brought the brandy he explained in Dutch, and then asked, 'Is Nurse here yet?'

'Any minute now.'

'She must cope here while you take Emma back to your house. Stay with her for as long as you need to, get her a hot drink and try to get her to lie down.' Then, in English, he said, 'Drink this, Emma. Juffrouw Smit will take you back to her house in a moment. Leave the letter with me. I will telephone Mr Trump and discover all I can, then let you know what is best to be done.'

'I must go...'

'Of course. Don't worry about that. I'll arrange everything. Now, drink the rest of the brandy like a good girl.'

A little colour had crept into her cheeks and he took her hands in his.

'Do as Juffrouw Smit suggests and wait until I come, Emma.' His quiet voice pierced her numb senses, firm and comforting, letting her know that he would do everything he could to help her. She gave him a small bleak smile and went with Juffrouw Smit.

There were five minutes before his patient would arrive, and the doctor spent them sitting at his desk. By the time she was ushered in by the nurse he knew exactly what had to be done.

Emma, like an obedient child, did just what Juffrouw Smit bade her do: drank the tea she was offered and lay down on her bed with a blanket tucked around her. She was aware that Juffrouw Smit was talking to her in a quiet, comforting voice, sitting by the bed holding her hand. Presently, she told herself, she would think what must be done, but somehow her thoughts slid away to nothing...

She had no idea how long she had been lying there when Dr van Dyke came in.

Juffrouw Smit slipped away and he sat down in her chair and took Emma's hand in his. She opened her eyes and looked at him, and then sat up in bed as the realisation of what had occurred penetrated her shock.

'Mother,' she said, and burst into tears...

The doctor sat on the bed beside her and took her in his arms again and let her cry until she was exhausted. When she had finally come to a stop, he mopped her face and said, 'There's my brave girl—and you must stay brave, Emma. I shall take you over to England this evening. We shall go to Mr Trump's house, where you will stay for a few days. He will help you and advise you and make all the necessary arrangements. So, now I want you to come downstairs and eat something and pack a bag. We shall leave here as soon after five o'clock as possible.'

She peered at him through puffy eyelids. 'Am I not to come back here?'

'Of course you're coming back. I shall come over and fetch you. But we will talk about that later. Just take enough with you for five or six days. I'm going to take Percy with me now; he will stay with Prince and Kulk until you come back.'

'Did you phone Mr Trump? I'm sorry to give you so much trouble...'

'Yes, I rang him and he is expecting you to stay. Don't worry, Emma, he will explain everything to you this evening.'

'But you can't leave here—your patients, the hospital...'

'Leave that to me.' He gave her a reassuring

pat on the shoulder. 'I'm going now. Be ready for me shortly after five o'clock.'

For Emma the day was endless. She packed her overnight bag, did her best to swallow the food Juffrouw Smit offered her and tried to think sensibly about the immediate future. But time and again her thoughts reverted to her mother and the awful suddenness of it all. She wanted desperately to know exactly what had happened. Perhaps she wouldn't feel so grief-stricken once she knew that. She knew it was useless, but she longed to run from the house and go back to England without wasting a moment.

But five o'clock came at last and she stood ready to leave the moment the doctor came for her. She neither knew or cared how she got to Mr Trump; the doctor had said he would see to everything and she had thought no more about it.

When she had been waiting for ten minutes he finally came, but her nerves were on edge and when Juffrouw Smit offered him coffee and something to eat she could have screamed at the delay.

He took a quick look at her tense face, declined the offer and picked up her case. He was tired and hungry, for he had spent time arranging their journey as well as doing his hospital round and then leaving his registrar to deal with anything urgent.

Emma bade a hasty goodbye to Juffrouw Smit and made for the door, impatiently listening to the doctor telling his secretary that he would be there in the morning for his patients. He spoke in Dutch, but as far as Emma was concerned it could have been any language under the sun; if only they could start their journey...

She wondered from where they would get a ferry—and surely it would be far into the night before they got to Mr Trump's house?

As though he had read her thoughts, Dr van Dyke said, 'Just a short drive. There's a plane waiting for us at Schipol; we will be at Heathrow in an hour or so.'

She hardly noticed anything of their journey; she was deeply thankful that she would be back in England so quickly, and at any other time she would have been thrilled and delighted at the speed with which they travelled, but now all she could think of was to get to Mr Trump as quickly as possible.

It seemed perfectly natural that a car should be waiting at Heathrow. She had thanked the pilot when they left the plane and hardly noticed the ease with which they went from it to the car.

The doctor, who had had very little to say on their journey, asked now, 'You know where Mr Trump lives? I have his address but I am not familiar with Richmond.'

Half an hour later they were sitting in Mr Trump's drawing room, drinking coffee while his wife plied them with sandwiches. To her offer of a bed for the night the doctor gave a grateful refusal. 'I've arranged to fly back at eleven o'clock; I have appointments I cannot break in the morning.'

The quiet normality of Mr Trump's home had restored some of Emma's habitual calm. 'But you can't,' she declared. 'You'll be tired. Surely there is someone who could take over for you…?'

She wished she hadn't said that; he had gone to a great deal of trouble to get her to Mr Trump but of course he wanted to get back to his home and his practice as soon as possible. She had disrupted his day most dreadfully.

She said quickly, 'I'm sorry. Of course you know what is best. I'm very grateful—I can never thank you enough… Of course you must go back home as quickly as possible.'

The doctor got up to go. 'I shall be back for your mother's funeral, Emma.' He took her hands in his. 'Mr Trump will take care of everything for you.' He bent and kissed her cheek. 'Be a brave girl, my dear.'

He shook hands with Mrs Trump and went out of the room with Mr Trump. The two men had talked on the phone at some length during the day, and now the doctor said, 'I will arrange things so that I can get here for the funeral and stay for several days. It is very good of you to have Emma to stay.'

'My wife and I are very fond of her, and we have always thought that she had less fun out of life than most girls. She was splendid when her father died. There's Salcombe to decide about, of course.'

'If you think it a good idea I'll drive her there.'

'That might be a very good idea. I'm grateful to you for getting her here so quickly.'

They shook hands and the doctor drove back to Heathrow and was flown back to Schipol, to get thankfully into his car and take himself home. Tomorrow he would get his plans made so that he could go back to England for as long as Emma needed him.

Mr Trump vetoed Emma's request for an account of her mother's death. 'You are tired,' he told her. 'Go to bed and sleep—for I'm sure that you will, whatever you think. In the morning we will sit quietly and I will tell you all that I know. I can promise you that your mother and her friend died instantly; they would have known nothing.'

Emma, worn out by grief and the nightmare day, went to her bed and fell at once into exhausted sleep.

Facing her as she sat opposite him in his study the next morning, Mr Trump saw that she was composed and capable of listening to what he had to say. 'I will tell you exactly what happened, and then we must discuss what arrangements you will wish to be made...'

It was almost a week later, on the evening before her mother's funeral, that Emma went into Mr Trump's drawing room and found Dr van Dyke there.

He got up and went to her at once and took her hands in his.

'Emma—how are you? Mr Trump tells me that you have been such a help to him...'

'Have you come...? That is, will you be here tomorrow?'

'Yes. Mr Trump and I have talked it over and he agrees with me that, if you agree, I should drive you down to Salcombe after the funeral. You will have several matters to deal with there.'

'Oh, would you do that? Thank you.' She found her hands were still in his and withdrew them gently. 'But you will want to get back to Holland...'

'No, no. I don't need to return for several days. Ample time in which you can attend to matters.' He smiled down at her. 'When everything is settled to your satisfaction, I'll take you back to Amsterdam.'

Mrs Trump bustled in then. 'Had your little chat?' she asked comfortably. 'I'll bring in the tea tray; I'm sure we could all do with a cup.'

The doctor went after tea, saying that he would be back in the morning. The funeral was to be at eleven o'clock and he proposed driving Emma down to Salcombe shortly afterwards. From what Mr Trump had told him there would be small debts to pay in the town, and an interview with the bank manager.

'I suspect,' Mr Trump had said thoughtfully, 'that there is no money—indeed, there may be an overdraft. Of course, the bank were not able to tell me this on the phone, but I feel I should warn you.'

'Will you let me know if there is any difficulty? You may count on me to deal with any.'

Mr Trump had given him a sharp glance. 'I don't think that Emma would like to be in your debt, even though you have proved yourself to be such a good friend.'

The doctor had only smiled.

It was a grey afternoon by the time he drove away from Mr Trump's house with a silent Emma beside him. The funeral had been quiet; there were no close relatives to attend, although there had been friends who had known her mother when she had lived at Richmond. They had been kind to Emma, saying all the right things but careful not to ask as to her future. It had only been the Trumps who'd wished her a warm goodbye, with the assurance that she was to come and stay with them whenever she felt like it. And Mr Trump had added that she could count on him for advice and help in any way.

There was no will; her mother had delayed making one, declaring that making a will was a morbid thing to do, and he had explained that there might be very little money.

'The cottage will be yours, of course, and I'll see to that for you, and its contents, but I know of nothing else. You will need to see your bank manager... Ask him to get in touch with me if there are any difficulties.'

So Emma had a lot to think about, but the first muddle of her thoughts must be sorted out, so it was a relief when the doctor said cheerfully, 'Do you want to talk? Perhaps you would rather have your thoughts?'

'I've had them all week,' said Emma bleakly, 'and they've got me nowhere.'

'Then think them out loud; perhaps I can help?'

'You've done so much already. I can never repay you.' All the same she went on, 'I've forgotten to do so much. The cottage—I should have written to Mrs Pike, who used to clean it for us—and asked her to go and turn on the water and the electricity; it's always turned off when there is nobody there...'

'That's been dealt with,' he told her, 'and there will be food in the fridge and the beds made.'

'Oh, did Mrs Trump think of it? She's been so kind.'

He didn't correct her. 'So that's one problem settled. What's next?'

Slowly, all her doubts and fears came tumbling out, but she stopped short at her biggest fear: her own future. The doctor hadn't said any more about her going back to Amsterdam and she could hardly blame him; she had been enough trouble to him. But if, as Mr Trump had hinted, there wasn't much money in the bank, she would have to find work quickly. 'What about Percy?' she asked suddenly.

'I left him in splendid spirits. He and Prince are devoted; he even climbs into Prince's basket and sleeps with him. They may not look alike but they are obviously soul mates.'

It was on the tip of her tongue to observe that they would miss each other when Percy came back to England, but she stopped herself in time; the doctor might think she was trying, in a roundabout way, to find out if he intended to employ her. Instead she said, 'I must see to things at the cottage.' A task she dreaded—sorting out her mother's possessions, her clothes, looking through her papers.

'Only after you have seen your bank manager and Mr Trump has advised you.'

He gave her a quick sideways glance. 'Mr Trump told me how splendidly you coped when your father died; you will cope splendidly now, Emma.'

They were on the A303 by now, going fast through an early dusk, but as a roadside service station came into sight he slowed.

'Tea, don't you think? We still have quite a way to go.'

Over tea and toasted teacakes she asked him anxiously, 'You don't have to drive back this evening, do you? And won't you be too late for the evening ferry? I didn't think—I'm sorry I've made things so difficult for you.'

'Not at all. I'm staying at Salcombe until you've got things settled as you want them.'

'Staying in Salcombe? But it might be days...'

'Don't worry, I've taken a week or so off.' He smiled at her across the table—such a kind smile that her heart gave a happy little skip; he would be there, helpful and self-assured, knowing what had to be done and how to do it. She smiled widely at him. 'Oh, how very nice—and how kind of you. It will be all the quicker with two, won't it?'

He agreed gravely and passed his cup for more tea, and Emma, feeling happier than she had done for days, bit with something like an appetite into her toasted teacake.

It was a dark evening by the time he parked the Rolls by the pub, took out her case and his own, and went with her to the cottage. He took the key from her and opened the door, switched on the lights and ushered her inside.

There were logs ready to light in the small fireplace, and he put a match to them before she had closed the door, and although the little room was chilly it was cheerful.

'While you put the kettle on,' he said briskly, 'I'll take the cases up. Which was your room?'

'On the left... Cases? But there's only my overnight bag—the case is in the car.'

He was halfway up the narrow stairs. 'I'll have the other room.' He looked over his shoulder at her surprised face. 'Did you really suppose that I would dump your things and leave you on your own?'

'Well,' said Emma, 'I don't think I'd thought about it.' She paused. 'No, that's not true. I've been dreading being alone here. I thought you would have booked a room in one of the hotels and driven back in the morning.'

'You must think me a very poor-spirited friend. But now we've cleared the matter up, go and make the tea; while we drink it we will decide what we will cook for supper.'

She took off her coat and went into the kitchen. She put the kettle on and got a teapot and mugs, then peered into the fridge. There was milk there, eggs and butter, bacon and a small loaf of bread.

'There's bacon and eggs and bread and butter,' she told him as he came into the kitchen, and he saw with relief that the shadow of sorrow had lifted from her face. She was pale and tired and unhappy, but the sharpness of her grief had been melted away by familiar surroundings and his matter-of-fact acceptance of events. Without thinking about it, she had accepted his company as a perfectly natural thing. Which was what he had hoped for.

She cooked their supper presently, while he laid the table, and when they had washed up they sat by the fire talking. There were plans to be made but he wouldn't allow her to get too serious about them. Beyond agreeing with her that seeing the bank manager was something which needed to be done as soon as possible, he began to discuss what groceries they would need to buy and the necessity of visiting Mrs Pike.

It was only much later, when she was in bed and on the edge of sleep, that she remembered that if she was to stay in Salcombe she wouldn't need that lady's services. And tomorrow, she promised herself, she would ask the doctor if he still wished to employ *her*.

She was awakened by his cheerful bellow urging her to come down to the kitchen and have her early-morning tea. She had slept all night, and although at the moment of waking she had felt a remembering grief, it was no longer an unbearable ache. She dragged on her dressing gown and went downstairs, and found the doctor, in a vast pullover, with his hair uncombed and a bristly chin, pouring the tea into mugs. His good morning was cheerfully impersonal. 'I can see you've slept well. While you drink your tea I'll go and shave.'

'Have you been up long? I didn't hear you.'

'Proof that you slept well; your shower is the noisiest I've ever come across. While you cook breakfast I'll go and get some rolls; they should be hot from the oven.'

It was a cold bright morning when, after breakfast, they walked through the town to the bank. At its door Emma said hesitantly, 'Would you mind coming with me? I'm sure there's nothing I can't understand or deal with, but just in case there's something…'

The manager received them gravely, uttering the established condolences, enquiring after Emma's health, and acknowledging the doctor's presence with a thoughtful look. He opened the folder on his desk and coughed.

'I'm afraid that what I have to tell you is of a rather disturbing nature, although I am sure we can come to some decision together. There was a small sum of money in your joint account with your mother to which you added before you went to Holland. Not a great deal of money, but sufficient to give your mother a modicum of security. She had her pension, of course, and she gave me to understand that she had no need to contribute to household expenses so that the pension was an adequate amount for her personal needs. Unfortunately she spent her money freely, and when the account was empty per-

suaded me to allow her an overdraft, assuring
me that you would repay it. In short, she spent
a good deal more than the overdraft and there
are a number of debts outstanding.'

Emma asked in a small shocked voice, 'But
what could she have spent the money on? Her
pension was enough for clothes and spending
money—there was a few hundred in our account. Are you sure?'

'Quite sure. I'm sorry, Miss Dawson, but I
was assured by your mother that there were
funds she could call upon, and since I have
known your parents for a number of years I saw
no reason to question that.'

'Besides the bank, do you know to whom she
owed money?'

'I hold a number of cheques which the bank
have refused to pay. It would be quite in order
for you to have them and settle them personally.
I suggest that I should open an account here in
your name so that you can settle the accounts
at your convenience.'

'But I haven't...' began Emma, but was
stopped by Dr van Dyke's calm voice.

'That is sound advice, Emma. Allow Mr
Ansty to open a new account in your name, and
perhaps he would be good enough to tell me
how much is needed to cover any payments.'
When Emma opened her mouth to protest, he

said, 'No, Emma, allow me to deal with this for the moment.'

There was something in his voice which stopped her saying anything more. Only she gave a little gasp when Mr Ansty told the doctor how much was needed to cover the debts and the overdraft. After that she didn't listen while the two men dealt with it, for her mind was wholly occupied with the ways and means of paying back so vast a sum. How on earth was she going to do it?

It wasn't until they were out on the street again that she stopped suddenly.

'I must be mad—whatever have I let you do? We must go back and tell him that you've changed your mind.'

The doctor said nothing, but whisked her into the nearby patisserie and ordered coffee.

'Didn't you hear what I said?' hissed Emma.

'Yes, I did. And when we get back to the cottage I will explain everything to you. Now, drink your coffee like a good girl and we will do the shopping.'

He sounded matter-of-fact, and quite unworried, and that served to calm her down a little. All the same, going in and out of the shops buying their lunch and supper, and listening politely to sympathetic condolences, at the back of her mind was the uneasy feeling that she wasn't quite sure what was happening...

There was a message on the answerphone from Mr Trump when they returned to the cottage. Mrs Riddley's niece would be driving down to Salcombe on the following day to collect her aunt's possessions. She hoped that Miss Dawson had left everything untouched so that she could check for herself that everything was as it should be.

'Well, really,' exclaimed Emma crossly. 'Does she suppose I'd take anything which wasn't Mother's?' She sliced bread with a good deal of unnecessary energy. 'And do I have to stay here all day waiting for her?'

'Very likely. And I must go to the medical centre tomorrow. What's for lunch?'

'Welsh Rarebit. I must go and see Mrs Pike and Miss Johnson...' She was buttering toast. 'And you are going to explain to me about paying the bills.'

He had intended to explain a good deal more than that, but as they finished their meal there was a knock on the door and there was Mrs Craig standing on the doorstep, expecting to be asked in.

'I heard you were here.' She looked at Dr van Dyke, 'With the doctor. I had to come to see you to express my sympathy and have a little chat. I saw your mother frequently, you know, and I'm sure you would wish to know what a happy life she was leading. Such a sad thing to happen, and you so far from her at the time, although I hear that she died instantly.'

Mrs Craig settled herself comfortably in a chair. 'I would have gone to the funeral if it had been here, but of course she wished to be buried with her husband.'

She doesn't mean to be unkind, thought Emma, sitting rigid in her chair, but if she doesn't go soon I shall scream.

It was the doctor who came to the rescue. 'You are the very person we wanted to see,' he told Mrs Craig. 'May I come back with you to the hotel? There is someone there I believe had dealings with Mrs Dawson, and it would make it so much easier if you could introduce me. I'm sure you must know her...'

Mrs Craig got up at once. 'Of course, Doctor. I'm so delighted to be of help. I've lived here for some time now and know almost everyone here. Emma, you will forgive me if I don't stay, for I'm sure Dr van Dyke is anxious to settle his business.'

Emma was left alone, to cry her eyes out in peace, so that when the doctor came back she was tolerably cheerful again, in the kitchen getting their tea.

'There were one or two small bills at the hotel,' he told her. 'I've settled them.' He didn't tell her that he had telephoned Mr Trump, paid a visit to the rector and talked at length with Kulk.

When she suggested again that they had to talk about his arrangements with the bank he brushed it aside. 'You have had enough to think about today,' he told her. 'We will get a meal at the pub and not be too late in bed, for we don't know how early this niece will arrive.'

They ate fresh-caught fish and a mountain of chips, and since there was no one else in the little dining room behind the bar the landlord came and talked to them while they ate, gathering up their plates when they had finished and promising them apple pie and cream.

The doctor kept up a casual flow of talk during their meal, urged her to have a brandy with her coffee and walked her briskly back to the cottage. She was pleasantly sleepy by now, and needed no urging to go to her bed. Tomorrow they would have that talk, and once Mrs Riddley's niece had taken her aunt's things she would pack away her mother's possessions. That left only Mrs Pike to see...

She woke in the small hours and sat up in bed, struck by a sudden thought. What a fool I am, she reflected. I can sell the cottage and pay back the money. I must tell him in the morning.

She fell asleep again, satisfied that the problem was solved.

They had barely finished breakfast when Mrs Riddley's niece arrived. Emma disliked her on sight; she was a youngish woman, fashionably thin, expensively dressed and skilfully made-up.

She answered Emma's polite greeting with a curt nod. 'You're Emma Dawson? I haven't much time; I intend to drive back as soon as possible.' She went past Emma into the cottage. 'I hope you haven't touched any of my aunt's possessions...'

Emma said quietly, 'No. I'm sorry that Mrs Riddley died.'

The doctor, at the kitchen sink, rattled a few plates.

'Someone else is here?'

'A friend who brought me back to England. Would you like coffee, or would you prefer to go straight to your aunt's room?'

'Oh, I'll get her stuff packed up first. Which room is it?'

'I'll show you, and when you are ready perhaps you will look around the cottage and make sure that there is nothing you have overlooked?'

'Certainly I shall.' She closed the door firmly in Emma's face.

The doctor was drying plates with the air of one who had been doing it all his life. He lifted an eyebrow at Emma as she went into the kitchen.

'Keep a sharp eye on her; she might filch the spoons!'

Emma, a bit put out, giggled, feeling suddenly light-hearted.

After a while the niece came downstairs. 'I've packed up my aunt's things. There are several dresses and hats too old to bother with. I dare say you can take them to a charity shop.'

She looked at the doctor, all at once smiling.

'Dr van Dyke—this is Miss or is it Mrs Riddley?' said Emma. 'And actually I think you should take everything with you.'

'Oh, undoubtedly,' said the doctor smoothly. 'One needs to be careful about these matters. I'll fetch a plastic sack and you can bundle everything in it.'

'Would you like coffee?' asked Emma. 'And then you must go round the cottage.'

Miss Riddley refused coffee. 'I left the car at the end of the quay...'

'I'll carry your bags to it,' offered the doctor. 'We will let Mr Trump know that you have been and removed everything of your aunt's.' He stood up. 'Shall we go? I dare say you are anxious to get back home?'

Chilling good manners, thought Emma, watching Miss Riddley mince along on her high heels beside the doctor. He looks very nice from the back, reflected Emma, and then she thought, I'll tell him about selling the cottage and how I'll pay back his money, and then he can go back to Amsterdam and not feel he has to do anything more for me. Of course there's Percy. Perhaps he wouldn't mind giving me a lift back so that I can bring Percy back here...

Much taken with this half-witted idea, she went upstairs to make quite sure that Mrs Riddley's possessions had really gone.

There was no sign of the doctor when she went back downstairs and she remembered that he had intended to go to the medical centre. She had her coffee and started on a task she had been putting off: going through the desk her mother had used and clearing out the papers in it. It was something which had to be done, and it seemed likely that now everything was more or less settled the doctor would wish to return to Holland. That was something else she must talk to him about without delay. She had been living in a kind of limbo, doing what he suggested, not allowing herself to think too much about the future, but it was time she faced up to that.

She finished clearing the desk and set the table for lunch, which would be cheese and pickles and the rolls he had fetched early that morning—there was to be no lingering over lunch, she decided. There was too much to talk about.

But she wasn't to have her wish. The doctor came in briskly, observed that he had seen the niece drive away and then gone to see his former colleagues, then added as a kind of afterthought, 'What do you call me, Emma?'

'Call you? Why, Dr van Dyke.'

'My name is Roele.'

'Yes, I know, but I can't call you that; I've been working for you. Which reminds me...'

He gave her no chance to continue. 'Yes, you can.' He sat back in his chair and smiled at her. 'Will you marry me, Emma?'

She put the roll she was buttering back on her plate, staring at him.

'Why?' she asked.

He was amused, but all he said was, 'A sensible question. I am thirty-six, Emma. I need a wife to run my home, entertain my friends and—er—support me.'

'But Kulk runs your home beautifully and your friends might not like me. Besides, you don't need supporting. Indeed, you've been supporting me.' She added politely, 'Thank you for asking me. I've had a very good idea this morning. I shall sell the cottage and then I can pay you back all that money you gave the bank.'

'And?'

'Then I'll get a job.'

'For such a sensible girl you have some odd ideas, Emma. What job? And where will you live? And how will you pay the rent and feed yourself on the kind of wages you are able to earn?'

'Well, I must say,' said Emma crossly, 'I thought you'd be pleased to be free to go back home.' She frowned. 'This is a very strange conversation.'

'Indeed it is. Shall we start again. Will you marry me, Emma?'

CHAPTER SEVEN

SHE stared at him across the table. 'But you don't—that is, you can't possibly be in love with me...'

'I have made no mention of love, or falling in love, Emma. Indeed, a happy marriage is as likely to be the result of compatibility, a real liking for each other, and the slow growing of deep affection which would surely follow. Sound bases on which to build. Whereas all too often marrying on impulse whilst in the throes of a love which so often turns into infatuation turns into disaster.'

He smiled at her. 'Do I sound like an elder brother giving you advice? I don't mean to; I'm only trying to make the situation clear to you without pretending to a romance that doesn't exist.'

'And if I should say yes?'

'We will marry as soon as possible and go back to Amsterdam. You will, of course, keep this cottage. We both like Salcombe, don't we?

And it would be nice to keep a foot in the door here.'

'Have you ever been in love?' asked Emma. If he was surprised at her question he didn't show it.

'Oh, countless times. Young men do, you know, it's all part of growing up. And you?'

'Oh, yes. With film stars and the music master at school and my best friend's brother—only they went to live abroad and I forgot about him. And of course there was Derek, but I didn't love him—only got used to him. Mother liked him and he was always very attentive—until Father died and he discovered that he was bankrupt and it would damage his career if he married me. Would I damage *your* career?'

He answered her with perfect gravity. 'No. Indeed, I suppose it would be a great advantage to me. A married man always seems so much more reliable!'

'You might meet someone and fall in love… So might I…'

'There is that possibility, but remember that I am no longer an impetuous youth and you, if I may say so, have reached the age of reason.'

'I'm twenty-seven,' snapped Emma, 'and if you suppose that I'm a staid spinster you're mistaken.'

'No, no, I wouldn't imagine anything of the

sort. I merely meant to imply that we are both of us ideally suited to be man and wife.'

'You're not asking me because you are sorry for me?'

His, 'Good Lord, no,' had a satisfyingly genuine ring to it. All the same she frowned.

'Ought we to wait and think about it?'

'For my part, I've done my thinking, but by all means take all the time you need, Emma. I'll go back to Amsterdam in a while, and you can make up your mind at your leisure.'

This was a prospect she didn't fancy; to be here in the cottage on her own and Roele not there to advise her... But of course she couldn't ask his advice about marrying him, could she?

'You don't know anything about me...'

'On the contrary, I know that you are capable, sensible, have similar tastes and interests to mine, you are a good listener, have the ability to face up to life, and, as a bonus, you are a very attractive young woman. And let me make it quite clear to you that I do not wish for or expect you to strive for a romantic attachment until such time as you feel ready for it.'

'Just friends to start with?'

'You see what I mean? Sensible and matter-of-fact. Just friends—good friends.'

'There's another thing. I think you must be

comfortably off, but I want you to know that I'm not marrying you for your money.'

Roele gave a small inward sigh of relief. His darling Emma was going to marry him, and sooner or later would learn to love him. In the meantime he had more than enough love for them both. He said firmly, 'I know you aren't, and, yes, I do have rather a lot of money. It will be nice to share it with someone.'

His smile was warm and friendly and utterly reassuring. 'Will you marry me, Emma?'

'Yes, I will. I like you very much and I know that I would miss you very much if you were to go away, and—and when you're not here I feel a bit lost. Only I hope I won't be a disappointment to you.' She looked at him with a question in her eyes. 'You would tell me?'

'Yes, I promise you that I will.' He leaned across the table and took one of her hands in his. 'Would you object to getting married by special licence as soon as possible? Here in Salcombe? And we'll return to Amsterdam as soon as possible afterwards.'

'I still have Mother's things to pack up...'

'Then start on that while I go and see Mrs Pike and talk to the rector.'

'Does it take a long time to get a special licence?'

'It should be in the post tomorrow morning; all we need to do is fix a time and a day.'

'Just us?'

'Well, I think Dr Walters might like to be at the church, and what about Miss Johnson and Mrs Craig?'

'Oh, witnesses. Of course. All right. And now everything is settled we had better get started.'

She got up and began to clear the table, but he took the dishes out of her hands and put his hands on her shoulders. 'How very unromantic of me to propose to you over the remnants of a meal. I must make up for that...' He bent and kissed her gently. 'We shall be happy, Emma, I promise you...'

His kiss sent a glow of warmth through her; she was honest enough to admit that she enjoyed it, and for the first time since her mother's death she felt a surge of content and happiness.

As soon as he had gone in search of the rector and Mrs Pike she went to her mother's room and began the sad task of packing up her clothes.

The cupboards and drawers were stuffed full. In the short time in which Emma had been away Mrs Dawson had indeed spent a good deal of money on dresses, hats and shoes—most of them hardly worn. They would have to go to a charity shop.

She picked out one or two of the more sober garments in case Mrs Pike might like to have them, bundled everything else in sacks and then opened her mother's jewel box. There was a pearl necklace, rings and brooches and earrings. They were hers now, Emma supposed. She closed the box. She would wear the pearls on her wedding day but the rest she would put away until an occasion when she might need to wear them.

She wept a little as she thought of her mother and father. I'm an orphan, she thought, drowning in sudden self-pity, until her sensible self took over again and she reminded herself that she was going to get married to a man she liked very much and go and live in a splendid house and share his life. And she was going to make a success of it too.

Roele came back then, with the news that the rector would marry them in two days' time at ten o'clock in the morning, if she was agreeable to that. And as for Mrs Pike, he had arranged for her to go to the cottage once a week and keep it in good order. 'For of course we shall come here from time to time, even if it is only for a few days. Now, what do you want me to do with your mother's clothes?' he asked.

She had been crying, poor girl. The quicker

the cottage was empty of things which would remind her of her grief the better.

'There are three sacks full. Could you take them to the charity shop? The nearest one is in Kingsbridge.'

'A good idea. Get your hat and coat; we'll both go. I'll take them along to the car while you get ready.'

By the time she had done that, and tidied her face and hair, she looked quite cheerful again. As they drove the few miles to Kingsbridge he kept up a steady flow of cheerful remarks, so that by the time they reached the shop and handed everything over she was quite ready to go to a tea room at the bottom of the high street and linger over tea and hot buttered crumpets.

They were married two days later, on a morning of tearing wind and persistent rain, despite which a surprising number of people came to the church to see them wed. Dr Walters and his colleagues, Miss Johnson and Phoebe, Mrs Craig and Mrs Pike, several members of the lifeboat crew, even the cross-looking baker's wife.

They gathered round when the simple cere-mony was over, offering good wishes and wav-ing goodbyes as they got into the Rolls. They drove through the little town and on to the road

to Exeter on the first stage of their journey back
to Holland.

They had had an early breakfast. Roele had
taken the luggage to the car and locked the cottage door with the cheerful remark that they
would be back in the spring, and then popped
her into the car and driven to the church without
giving Emma time to feel regret or sadness. And
now he kept up a steady flow of talk: the unexpected pleasure of seeing friends and acquaintances at the church, the stormy weather,
the pleasure of seeing Prince and Percy again.

'You won't see much of me for a few days,'
he told her. 'I'll have a backlog of work, but
that will give you time to get used to the house
and do some shopping. I should warn you that
the nearer we get to Christmas the more social
life there will be. Which will give you a chance
to meet my friends.'

'Oh, do you have a lot of friends and go out
a great deal?'

'Plenty of friends, yes. And I do have a social
life, but a very moderate one.'

They were on the A303, driving into wors-
ening weather. As they approached Middle
Wallop Roele said, 'We will stop for lunch.' He
turned to smile at her. 'Breakfast seems a long
time ago. There's rather a nice place where we
can get a meal.'

He took a side-turning and stopped before a handsome manor house on the edge of a village. After the gloomy skies and heavy rain its comfortable warmth was welcoming. Emma, led away by a pleasant waitress, returned to find that Roele was sitting at the bar.

'I hope you're hungry; I am.' The bartender put two champagne cocktails before them. 'To our future together, Emma.'

It was probably the champagne which gave her such a pleasureable feeling of excitement.

They lunched on sauté mushrooms, duckling and orange sauce and bread and butter pudding and a pot of delicious coffee. Looking out at the wild weather, Emma felt very reluctant to leave.

'I'll phone from the car,' Roele told her. 'I doubt if the Harwich Ferry will be running in this weather. If that's the case, we'll make for Dover.'

It was the case; the Harwich Ferry was cancelled. But the Dover ferries were still running, so the doctor drove on to the M25 and presently took the Dover road.

It was well into the afternoon now, and already getting dark with no sign of the weather improving. Emma, sitting in the car, waiting to go on board the ferry, looked at the rough seas and hoped for the best.

On board, she drank the tea she was offered

and opened the magazine Roele had bought her.
They should be home by midnight, he assured
her. It was a long drive to Amsterdam, but the
roads were good and fast and Kulk would be
waiting for them. She smiled and nodded and
tried not to notice the heaving deck. They were
halfway across when she put the magazine
down.

'I'm going to be sick,' said Emma.

The doctor took a quick look at her white
face, heaved her gently to her feet and led her
away. And she, feeling truly awful, wouldn't
have cared if he had thrown her overboard.

Instead he dealt with things with an impersonal kindness which made it less awful than it
was, finally gently washing her face and settling
her in her seat again with an arm round her. He
made her drink the brandy the steward brought,
then tucked her head onto his shoulder. 'Go to
sleep,' he told her, 'we are nearly there. Once
we're on land you'll be quite yourself again. My
poor girl, I should never have brought you—we
should have stayed until tomorrow.'

Emma mumbled into his coat, feeling better
already. 'That wouldn't have done; you told me
that you had an appointment tomorrow.' She
hiccoughed as a result of the brandy, and closed
her eyes. She was quite safe with Roele's arm
around her, and not only safe but happy.

He was right, of course, once on dry land she was quite herself again. It was dark night now, the rain lashing down, blown hither and thither by the wind, but the road was good and almost empty of traffic. Roele drove fast, relaxed behind the wheel of the big car, not saying much, only telling her from time to time where they were—along the coast to Ostend and then inland onto the E40. He turned off again onto the motorway to Antwerp, and then over the border into Holland to Utrecht and finally the outskirts of Amsterdam.

But before they reached the city the doctor turned off to go to his home, driving slowly now along the narrow road until he reached the village and a moment later drew up before his front door. There were lights shining out from the downstairs windows and the front door opened wide to reveal more light, with Kulk and Mevrouw Kulk standing there.

The doctor got out, opened Emma's door and swept her into the house through the rain and wind, to be greeted by handshaking and beaming smiles and a rush of excited talk. She was borne away by Mevrouw Kulk to have her coat taken, and ushered into the cloakroom at the back of the hall. She was tired and very hungry, and the prospect of bed was enticing, but she washed her face to wake herself up, tidied her hair and went back in to the hall.

Kulk was bringing in their luggage and Roele had gone out again to put the car in the garage. She stood for a moment, feeling uncertain. But only for a moment, for Mevrouw Kulk appeared through a door behind the staircase. With her was Percy, and close on his heels Prince.

Emma was kneeling on the floor, her arms round the two dogs, when the doctor came back. He threw his coat onto a chair, received the lavish affection offered by Prince and Percy and helped her to her feet.

'Welcome home, Emma. Mevrouw Kulk has a meal ready. You must be hungry—and longing for your bed. Sleep for as long as you like in the morning; I shall be away all day until early evening, forgive me for that, but the Kulks will look after you.'

He took her hand and led her through an arched double door into a room with a high-plastered ceiling and long windows. The walls were white and hung with paintings in heavy gilt frames, and the furniture matched the room—a rectangular mahogany table ringed by ribband-backed chairs, a massive sideboard bearing a display of silver, and a wide fireplace surmounted by an elaborate chimneypiece.

'This is a beautiful room,' said Emma, forgetting her tiredness for a moment as Roele sat her down at the table, where two places had been laid. Despite the lateness of the hour, she noted, silver and crystal gleamed on the lace tablemats and there were fresh flowers in a Delft blue bowl. And their supper, when it came, was delicious: beef bouillon, a creamy golden souf-flé and finally a fruit tart, the pastry light as a feather.

'And, since it is our wedding day, champagne is obligatory,' said the doctor. He smiled at her across the table. 'You were a beautiful bride, Emma.'

She gaped at him. 'In last year's suit and the only hat I could find in the town?'

'And still a beautiful bride. An unusual wedding day, perhaps, but I have enjoyed every minute of it.'

'Really? Well, yes, I suppose I have too—not the ferry, though!'

'I'm sorry about that too, but at least you will never forget your wedding day.' He studied her tired face. 'You would like to go to bed, wouldn't you? No coffee; it might keep you awake. Mevrouw Kulk shall take you to your room.' He got up and walked to the door with her, and bent and kissed her cheek. 'Sleep well, Emma.' After a pause, he added, 'I'll see to Percy.'

Already half asleep, she followed Mevrouw Kulk up the wide staircase, along a gallery and into a softly lit bedroom.

'I must explore it in the morning,' muttered Emma as Mevrouw Kulk drew curtains and opened doors and cupboards, switched on another bedside light and patted the turned-down coverlet before beaming with a *'wel te rusten'* as she went away.

Emma cleaned her teeth, washed her face, tore off her clothes and got into bed—to fall asleep instantly.

When she woke there was a sturdy young girl drawing back the curtains to reveal a dull morning. She sat up in bed and ventured a *'Goeden morgen'* with such success that the girl answered with a flood of Dutch.

Emma tried again. 'I don't understand' had been one of first useful phrases she had learnt. The girl smiled, picked up the tray she had set on the table under the window and brought it to the bed. Emma, struggling to find the words she wanted, was relieved to see a note propped up against the teapot. Roele in an almost unreadable scrawl, wished her good morning, recommended that she ate a good breakfast and then took the dogs for a walk, and said he would be home at about six o'clock.

Emma drank her tea, read the note again and

got up. The bathroom held every incentive to linger, with its deep bath and shelves loaded with towels, soap and everything else she could possibly want, but she resisted its luxury after a pleasurable time lying in a scented bath and dressed once more in the suit. Nicely made up, and with her hair in its usual topknot, she went downstairs.

Kulk was hovering in the hall to wish her good morning and lead her to the small room where she had breakfasted on her earlier visit. The table had been drawn near the brisk fire and Prince and Percy were waiting for her.

This was her home, she reflected as Kulk set a coffee pot down before her, moved the toast rack a little nearer and asked her if she would prefer bacon and eggs, scrambled eggs, or perhaps an omelette...

And I actually belong here, thought Emma, devouring the scrambled eggs with appetite and deciding that toast and marmalade would be nice, with another cup of coffee. She handed out morsels of toast to both dogs, and when Kulk came to see if there was anything else she would like she asked, 'The doctor, did he leave very early?'

His English was good, although the accent was pronounced. 'At half past seven, *mevrouw*. I understand he has a number of patients to see before going to the hospital, where he has a clinic and ward rounds.'

'You have been with the doctor for a long time?'

'I taught him to ride a bicycle, *mevrouw*, when I was a houseman at his parents' home. When they retired to a quiet life I came as his houseman and my wife as his cook.'

Emma set down her coffee cup. 'Kulk, this is all strange to me. I would be glad if you will help me…'

'With the greatest pleasure, *mevrouw*. Katje and I will do everything to assist you in any way. If you have finished your breakfast you might like to come to the kitchen and we will explain the running of the household to you. Katje speaks no English but I will translate, for you will wish to order the meals and inspect the linen and cutlery as well as the stores she keeps.'

'Thank you, Kulk. I should like to know as much as possible, but I have no intention of taking over.' She hesitated; Kulk was an old family servant and to be trusted. She said carefully, 'You see, Kulk, the doctor and I married without waiting for an engagement. I have recently lost my mother and I had no reason to stay in England.'

'Katje and I are happy that the doctor is hap-

pily married, *mevrouw*. For a long time we have
wished that, and now we are delighted to welcome you and serve you as we serve him.'

That sounded incredibly old-fashioned, but
she had no doubt that it was spoken in all sin-
cerity. 'Thank you—and Katje. May I call her
that? I know that I—we are going to be very
happy here. I'll come with you now, shall I?
May Prince and Percy come, too?'

'Of course, *mevrouw*.'

He led the way into the hall, through a door
beside the staircase and along a short passage
which led to the kitchen. This was a large room,
with windows overlooking the grounds behind
the house. It was old-fashioned at first glance,
but as well as the vast wooden dresser against
one wall and the scrubbed table at its centre
there was an Aga flanked by glass-fronted cupboards and shelves gleaming with shining
saucepans. There was a deep butler's sink under
one window and a dishwasher beside it, and on
either side of the Aga were two Windsor armchairs, each with a cat curled up on its cushion.

'The cats!' exclaimed Kulk. 'Perhaps you do
not care for them…?'

'Oh, but I do—and what a lovely kitchen.'

Mevrouw Kulk wasn't there, but she had
heard them for she called something to Kulk
from an open door in one wall. She came a mo-

ment later, holding a bowl of eggs. She put
them down, wished Emma good day and offered a chair.

Emma sat at the table, listening to Kulk talking to his wife, trying to understand what was
being said. But presently she gave up. As soon
as possible she would take lessons; her smattering of the language wouldn't be of much use
if she were to join in Roele's social life.
Besides, she would want to shop; he had never
mentioned her clothes, but she was quite sure
that as his wife she would be expected to dress
with some style.

Mevrouw Kulk interrupted her thoughts,
standing beside her with a pad and a pencil.

'Dinner for tonight,' said Kulk. 'Is there
something you would wish for? Katje has it
planned, but perhaps you would wish for other
things.'

'No, no, of course not. But I'd like to know
what we are to have…'

She left the kitchen after an hour with a good
idea of the day's routine kept by the Kulks.
There was a girl to help—she who had brought
her early-morning tea, Bridgette—and a gar-
dener, and once or twice a year local women
came in from the village to help with the bi-
annual cleaning of the house. 'If there is to be

a social occasion,' explained Kulk, 'then we get extra help.'

Obviously it was a well-run house which needed no help from her.

She put on a coat and went into the grounds with the dogs. There was a terrace behind the house, with steps leading down to a formal garden, and beyond that a great stretch of lovingly laid out shrubs and ornamental trees, and narrow stone paths with unexpected rustic seats and stone statues round every corner. Whoever had planned it had done it with meticulous attention to detail. She wandered round for some time, with Percy and Prince chasing imaginary rabbits and racing back to see if she was still there. It was a beautiful place even on a wintry morning; in summer it would be somewhere where one would want to sit and do nothing.

She went back indoors then and had the coffee Kulk had ready.

If *mevrouw* wished, he suggested, he would show her round the house. But perhaps she would prefer to wait for the doctor?

She thanked him. 'I would rather wait for the doctor to come home, and then we can go round it together, Kulk.'

'Quite right and proper, too,' said Kulk to Katje later, 'and them newlyweds and having plans and so forth. Such a nice young lady he's found for himself. Used to nice living, I can see that, but it must be very strange for her. A bit of help from us from time to time won't come amiss.'

There were books in the small sitting room, as well as newspapers in both Dutch and English. Besides that there was a television, discreetly tucked away in a corner. Emma, not easily bored, had plenty to keep her occupied, but after lunch she sat down by the fire, hemmed in by the dogs, and allowed her thoughts free rein.

It was apparent that Roele was more than just very well off, he had what her old schoolmistress had always referred to as 'background'— a background which, she suspected, stretched back for generations. She must ask him about that—but she must also remember not to plague him with endless questions for the time being. Having worked at his consulting rooms, she was aware of the number of patients he saw each day and the length of his visits to the hospital— more than one hospital, Juffrouw Smit had told her. Only when he had the leisure to talk to her would she question him.

There was a great deal unsaid between them, but she had expected that; they might have married, but they didn't know each other well. At least, she didn't know Roele, and she supposed that he didn't know her as a person. That they liked each other was a solid fact and that they would, in time, have a happy life together was something she didn't doubt. Until then she would be content...

She went upstairs to change into the jersey dress after tea, and when she came downstairs Roele was taking off his coat in the hall, fending off the dogs' delighted greeting. When he saw her he came to the bottom of the stairs and held out a hand.

'How nice to find you here, have you been bored or lonely?'

'Neither. It would be impossible to be lonely with the dogs, and I could never be bored in this house.'

'You have explored?'

'No.'

He was quick to see her hesitate. 'You waited for me? Splendid. We will go round now, and while we are having a drink before dinner you can tell me what you think of it.'

He put an arm round her shoulders and turned her smartly towards the big arched doorway on one side of the hall.

'The drawing room,' he said, and opened the door.

It was a large room, with walls hung with pale green silk between white-painted panels. There were brass sconces between the pillars and a cut-glass chandelier hung from the strap-work ceiling. The three tall windows were curtained in old-rose velvet and the floor was covered by a dark green Aubusson carpet with a floral design at its centre. Above the fireplace was an elaborate Rococo chimneypiece with an enormous mirror.

It was a very grand room, and its furniture reflected its grandeur: William and Mary settees on either side of the fireplace, two Georgian winged armchairs with a Pembroke table between them, a group of armchairs around a veneered rosewood tripod table and a scattering of small tables, each with its own lamp. There were two walnut display cabinets, filled with porcelain and silver, and a long-case clock facing the windows.

Emma stood in the middle of the room, taking it all in. 'What a wonderful room!' She caught sight of the pile of magazines and an open book lying on one of the tables. 'Do you use it often?'

'Oh, yes. It's remarkably cosy with a good fire burning in the winter. Tea round the fire on a Sunday afternoon with a good book and the right music. And for social occasions, of course.'

He crossed to the door and opened it. There was a conservatory beyond, and Emma lingered among the wealth of plants and shrubs before he ushered her through a further door and back into the hall. 'We've seen the dining room, now here is my study.' This proved to be another panelled room, its walls lined with bookshelves and a vast desk under its window.

Emma gazed around, wondering if she would be welcome in it. Probably not, she thought.

'You know the morning room,' said Roele, 'but there's one more room here.' He crossed the hall again and opened a door onto a quite small room, with two easy chairs by a small steel grate and a sofa table standing behind a big sofa under the window. 'My mother always used this room. She wrote her letters here and sat in that chair, knitting and working at her tapestry. I do hope you will make it your own, Emma.'

'Your mother?'

'She and my father live just outside Den Haag now. My father is retired—like me, he was a medical man—and they have a house in the country. We will go and visit them shortly.'

'Do they know that you married me?'

'Of course, and they are delighted to welcome you into the family.'

They were now halfway up the staircase, but she paused, her hand on the carved wood balustrade. 'If I were them,' she declared, letting grammar go to the winds, 'I wouldn't want to welcome me, coming in from nowhere—I might be an adventuress.'

The doctor laughed. 'An adventuress wouldn't have carroty hair,' he told her. 'Besides, they trust my judgement. Don't worry about them, Emma; they will like you and I think that you will like them.'

He led her across the gallery to the front of the house, opened a door and urged her inside. The room was large, with two tall windows opening out onto a wrought-iron balcony. A four-poster bed faced them, its coverlet in the same satin chintz as the curtains. There was a mahogany dressing table between the windows, with an elaborate carved framed triple mirror on it, a cabinet chest against one wall and a tallboy facing it. On either side of a small round table there were small tub chairs, and at the foot of the bed a Regency chaise longue. It was a beautiful room, and Emma said so.

'You must love your home, Roele,' she said.

'As you will love it too, Emma. We can go through here...' He led the way through a bathroom to a smaller room, simply furnished, and then out into the gallery again to open another door.

Emma lost count of the rooms after a time. When they had inspected those opening onto the gallery there were the side passages, leading to even more rooms, and then a staircase to the floor above.

'The nurseries,' said the doctor, sweeping her in and out of doors. Children's bedrooms, more guest rooms. And then up another staircase. 'Kulk and Katje have rooms here, and Bridgette too, and along here are the attics and a door onto the roof.'

There was a narrow parapet and an iron staircase down to the ground.

'We keep the door locked but the key hangs above it. Kulk has another key and so have I.'

'I had no idea...' began Emma.

He understood her at once. 'It is a large house, but it is also home—our home, Emma. You will learn to love it as I do.'

They went back downstairs and had drinks and a splendid dinner, and shortly afterwards Roele went to his study to work. Emma spent a blissful few hours in the drawing room, examining everything in it. Percy was with her, but Prince had gone with his master. Presently she was joined by the two cats, who wandered in and settled onto one of the settees with the air of welcome guests. That was what was so delightful about the house, reflected Emma, it *was* a home as well.

Roele came back then, asked her if there was

anything she would like before going to bed and suggested that she might like to go and see Juffrouw Smit on the following day. 'She would like you to go to her house for lunch. Kulk will drive you in about midday. I shall be at the hospital for most of the day, but I'll call for you at about half past one and bring you back here.'

He smiled at her. 'I shall be free at the week-end and we can be together. You're not too lonely?'

'No, of course not. There's such a lot to see. Tomorrow I had thought I'd walk to the village, but now I'm going to Juffrouw Smit, so I'll go to the village the next day. The days won't be long enough.'

She sounded so convincing that she almost convinced herself, and tried hard not to mind when he made no effort to keep her after she suggested that she should go to bed.

CHAPTER EIGHT

EMMA was relieved to see Juffrouw Smit's severe countenance break into a smile when she arrived for lunch the next day. It could have been an awkward meeting, but somehow her hostess gave the impression that she had expected Dr van Dyke and Emma to marry, and it was something of which she entirely approved.

'The doctor is coming for you at half past one so we do not have much time for a chat, but perhaps you will come again? I am interested to hear of your wedding and the cottage at Salcombe—as you know, the doctor has very little time to chat. A quiet wedding, I expect?'

So Emma sat down and drank very dry sherry and described her wedding; not that there was much to describe, but she made the most of it, enlarged upon their journey back and the awful weather, and, over lunch, described the cottage in detail.

'Perhaps you would like to stay there when you have a holiday? It is a charming little town and the people are friendly—besides, your English is so good.' She added impulsively, 'You were so kind to me when I came here to work for the doctor, and I never thanked you for that. But I do now. I'm glad I did work here, even in such a humble capacity, because now I can understand how hard Roele works.'

'You will be a good wife to him,' pronounced Juffrouw Smit. 'Now, we will have coffee here at the table, for the doctor will be here very shortly and I must go back to work. But you will come again, I hope?'

'Yes, please. There is such a lot I need to know—about the shops and all the everyday things one takes for granted in one's own country.'

Roele was punctual and she was glad that she was ready for him for, although he was his usual quiet self, she sensed that he was impatient to be back at work. So she shook hands with Juffrouw Smit, thanked her for her lunch without lingering and got into the car.

'I could have found my own way home,' she told him as they drove off.

'So you could, and I'll tell you how best to do that some time.' He smiled at her, thinking that she had called his house home quite unconsciously; they had been married for only a day or so and she was already fitting into his life as though it had been made for her. 'I'll be home earlier today,' he told her. 'We will have tea together and then take the dogs to the village.'

It was a short walk to the village. He took her to see the church, which was small and austere outside but the interior held high carved wood pews and a magnificent pulpit and its walls were covered by black and white marble plaques, many of them from Roele's family. And underfoot there were ancient gravestones, inscribed in flowery Latin. He showed her the front pew under the pulpit, with its red velvet cushions and hassocks. 'This is where we come on Sundays,' he told her.

The village was small, its little houses and cottages having shining windows and spotless paintwork. Here and there were larger houses, set haphazardly between the cottages. There was a small shop too, selling, as far as Emma could see, absolutely everything.

'And yet the village is so close to Amsterdam...'

'Yes, but off the beaten track, and a good many of the people living here are elderly and don't want the hassle of a bus ride to the shops. Come and meet Mevrouw Twist.'

The shop was dark inside, and it smelled of onions and of the smoked sausages hanging from the ceiling, with a whiff of furniture polish and washing powder. The doctor introduced her, bought dog biscuits and listened courteously to Mevrouw Twist's gossip, then shook hands, waited while Emma did the same, and then they went back into the small square.

'Tomorrow we have been asked to the *dominee's* house so that I may introduce you to him and his wife. In the evening at about six o'clock. We shall drink home made wine and stay for an hour.' He tucked her arm in his. 'You see, I lead two lives, Emma. I know everyone in the village but I have friends in Amsterdam, too.'

They were walking up the drive to the house, the dogs running ahead.

'Bear with me for a few more days and then we will go shopping. You always look nice, but you will need warm clothes and some pretty dresses...'

The following evening they walked to the *dominee's* house arm-in-arm, talking of everyday ordinary events, and Emma realised that she felt like a wife...

The *dominee* was tall and thin and rather earnest, while his wife was blonde, wholesomely good-looking and friendly. She took Emma away to see the baby—a boy, lying sleeping in

his cot. 'Roele is his godfather,' she told Emma.
She led the way into an adjoining room. 'Anna,
Sophia and Marijke,' she said and waved towards the three small girls sitting at the table,
schoolbooks spread around them.

Emma said hello, and their mother blew them
a kiss then took Emma back to the men. The
dominee gave her a glass of wine, saying, 'My
wife is clever; she makes the wine. This is from
rhubarb.'

He came and sat beside her. 'I am sorry to
hear that you have had a good deal of unhap-
piness, but now you are married to Roele you
will be happy again.'

'Yes, I know,' said Emma, and knew that that
was true.

Walking back presently, she told Roele, 'I
liked the *dominee* and his wife, and the baby
and the little girls. Have you known them for a
long time?'

'Years and years. He and I were at school
together. Jette is an old friend too.'

Towards the end of the week Roele told her
over dinner, 'I'll be free until the evening tomorrow. Shall we go shopping?'

Emma, heartily sick of the few clothes she
had brought with her, agreed with enthusiasm.

'You will need a winter coat and a good raincoat—get yourself whatever you wear in the

winter, and some pretty dresses for the evening and anything else you need.'

'Thank you, but how much may I spend?'

'You can use my account at some of the shops, but at the smaller shops I'll settle the bills as we go. I'll arrange for you to have an allowance as soon as possible, but in the meantime leave the paying to me.'

In bed that night, Emma thought uneasily that she needed a great deal, and that perhaps Roele hadn't realised how much even a basic wardrobe would cost him. But she had stayed awake worrying about that to no purpose; the next morning he drove her to Amsterdam, parked the car and walked her briskly to a street of small fashionable shops. The kind of shop, she saw, which displayed one or two mouthwatering garments in its narrow window with no price ticket in sight.

The doctor stopped before an elegant shop window. 'My sisters go here,' he observed, and ushered her into its dove-grey interior.

The elegant woman who glided towards them took in Emma's out-of-date but expertly tailored suit, the well polished equally out-of-date shoes and handbag, and recognised a good customer.

'Dr van Dyke—you were here with your sister some time ago.'

'Indeed I was. My wife would like some dresses. We shall be entertaining, so something for dinner parties.'

'I have the very thing for *mevrouw*, and so fortunate that a consignment of delightfully pretty outfits arrived only this week. If *mevrouw* will come with me?'

So Emma went behind elegant brocade curtains and had her useful suit and sweater taken from her and replaced by a dark green velvet dress, very plain, with long sleeves and a high neck, and a skirt which just skimmed her knees and showed off her shapely legs to great advantage.

She showed herself rather shyly to Roele, sitting comfortably in a gilt chair reading a newspaper.

'Very nice. Have it.'

'But I'm sure it's very expensive,' hissed Emma.

'Just right for dinner parties; get another one…blue…'

The saleslady had splendid hearing; she had a blue crêpe dress with short sleeves, a low square neck and a wide pleated skirt ready to slip over Emma's head.

When she went back to Roele again, he nodded. 'Very nice, have it, and get a couple of warm dresses…'

Emma, slightly light-headed, allowed herself to be fitted into a soft brown cashmere dress, and then a green jersey dress, a two-piece, and, since Roele approved of them both, she added them to the others. Once more in her old suit, she waited while Roele paid for everything and arranged for them to be sent round to his consulting rooms.

'We will pick them up before we go home,' he told her. 'Now, if I remember rightly there is a place here where they stock Burberry...'

With a short pause for coffee, Emma acquired a raincoat and hat, two tweed skirts she'd admired, a couple of cashmere sweaters and a handful of silk blouses. By then it was time for lunch.

Over lobster thermidor at Thysse and Dikker, she pointed out that she now had a splendid wardrobe—and shouldn't they go home?

'We are by no means finished,' the doctor pointed out. 'You need shoes, a couple of evening dresses, a wrap of some kind for the evening, a winter coat, a hat—for church—and undies. There's a small shop where my sisters always go, not too far away.'

Emma stopped worrying about the cost of everything, for it was obvious that Roele was unmoved by the bills. She bought shoes and slippers and boots, and a brown cashmere coat, and, after much searching, a plain, elegant felt hat with a narrow brim which she set at an angle on her carroty hair—the effect of which made the doctor stare so hard at her that she blushed and asked him if he didn't like it.

'Charming—quite charming!' he told her, and thought how beautiful she looked.

As for the undies, he left her for half an hour, and when he returned the saleswoman handed him a bag the size of which was evidence of her success in finding what she wanted.

He took her to an elegant little café for tea, and then presently drove to his consulting rooms, stowed her shopping in the boot and then drove home. Emma sat beside him, rehearsing the thank-you speech she intended to make once they were indoors. It had been a wonderful day, she reflected, and Roele appeared to have enjoyed it as much as she had. Let there be more days like this one, she prayed silently, doing things together...

She went to her room once they had reached the house, leaving Kulk to bring in the parcels while Roele stood in the hall, looking through the letters on the tray on the console table.

'I'll be down in a minute,' she told him, and flew upstairs to throw off her coat and tidy her hair, add a little lipstick and powder her nose. She was less than five minutes, and when she got downstairs again the doctor was still in his coat, talking to Kulk, who, when he saw her, tactfully slid away.

'Roele, thank you for a lovely day'—began Emma, to be interrupted.

'Delightful, wasn't it? I won't be in for dinner and don't wait up; I shall be late home. I'm glad you enjoyed the day; we must do it again some time.' He crossed the hall to her and bent and kissed her cheek. 'I won't be home until early morning; we can have breakfast together. Sleep well, Emma.'

She conjured up a smile and watched him go, her lovely day in shreds around her; he had probably hated every minute of it, but his beautiful manners had prevented him from showing his wish for the tiresome day to be over. And where was he going now, and with whom?

Emma felt a sudden and unexpected surge of resentment. And she felt ashamed of that, for he had been very patient with her and spent a great deal of money.

She went to find Katje and ask if she might have dinner a little earlier, so that she had time to spend the evening unpacking her clothes and trying them on before she went to bed. She even tried to explain what a splendid day she had had, and Katje nodded encouragingly and Kulk said what a pity it was that the doctor should have to spend the evening out of the house.

He shrugged his shoulders. 'But of course it is his work, *mevrouw*.'

So what right had she to feel so disgruntled? She told herself that she was becoming selfish and thoughtless.

After dinner she told Kulk that she would go to her room and would need nothing further that evening. 'The doctor told me that he would be very late back. Do you usually wait up for him?'

'No, *mevrouw*. Coffee and sandwiches are left ready for him and he lets himself into the house. I'll take Prince and Percy out for their final run, but the doctor doesn't like me to stay up later than midnight.'

Unpacking her new clothes and trying everything on took a long time. Emma was surprised to find that it was midnight by the time the last garment had been carefully hung away. She bathed and got ready for bed and then, on an impulse, went quietly down the stairs. The *stoel* clock in the hall chimed one as she reached it, dimly lit by a wall-light above the console table. She stood for a moment, listening. Perhaps Roele was in his study or the kitchen. But he was in neither. Only Prince and Percy, curled up together, lifted sleepy heads as she went into the kitchen.

There was coffee on the stove and a covered plate on the table. Sandwiches—slivers of ham between thin buttered slices of bread. Emma took one and sat down by the Aga to eat it. She was wearing her new dressing gown, pale pink quilted silk, her feet thrust into matching slippers, and she admired them as she ate. She wasn't sure why she had come down to the kitchen, but it was warm and comfortable and Roele might be glad of company when he got home. She took another bite of sandwich and turned round at the faint sound behind her.

Roele was standing in the doorway. He looked tired, but he was smiling.

'What a delightful surprise to find you here, Emma, eating my sandwiches...'

He came into the kitchen, acknowledging the dogs' sleepy greeting, and sat down opposite her.

'You don't mind? I don't know why I came down. Well, I suppose it was because I thought you might want to talk to someone. But I'll go back to bed if you don't want company.'

'My dear Emma, I am delighted to have company. But are you not tired?'

She was pouring coffee into two mugs and had put the sandwiches within his reach.

'Not a bit.' She sat down and added quietly, 'It was so kind of you to waste a whole day shopping with me. I enjoyed it, but all the while you must have been thinking about your patients and the hospital and wanting to be there.' Before he could speak she added, 'I want to thank you for everything, Roele. All my lovely clothes, and showing me the shops, and lunch and tea...'

It was tempting to tell her then that the day had been a delight for him too, that buying all the clothes she wanted had given him the greatest delight, and that if it were possible he would buy her the most splendid jewels he could find. But it was too soon; she was at ease with him, trusted him, but that was all. It was a strange situation, wooing Emma with a courtship after they were married, but he had no doubt of its success, provided he could possess his soul in patience.

He settled back in his chair and between sandwiches told her about the patient he had driven miles to see that evening: a public figure whose illness needed to be kept secret; even the faintest whisper of it would send the Stock Market into a state of chaos.

'He'll recover?'

'I believe so, and no one will be the wiser.'

He ate the last sandwich. 'How satisfying it is to come home to someone and talk.'

Emma took the mugs to the sink. 'Well, that's why we married, wasn't it, to be good companions?'

He got up, too. 'Yes, Emma. Is that thing you're wearing new? It's very pretty.' He kissed her cheek, a cool kiss which she had come to expect. 'Thank you for being here. Now go to bed and sleep. We will see each other at breakfast.'

She smiled at him sleepily, aware that something had happened between them although she had no idea what it was. In bed presently, she thought about it, but she was too sleepy to think clearly—knowing only that remembering the hour in the kitchen gave her a warm glow deep inside her.

She wore one of the cashmere jumpers and a new skirt to breakfast, and felt pleased when he remarked upon them.

'Will you be home for tea?' she asked him.

'I'll do my best. I've a clinic this afternoon, and sometimes we have to run overtime, but I'll be back in good time for dinner. I'll be free on Saturday, as well as Sunday, so we will go and see my mother and father. They are anxious to meet you. They wanted us to stay the night but I thought we might have Sunday to ourselves.

We'll go for lunch and stay for tea, and perhaps for dinner. We can take Percy and Prince.' He picked up his letters and came round the table to bend and kiss her. 'Have you any plans for today?'

'I'm to inspect the linen cupboard with Katje and then I'm going for a walk with the dogs.'

'Don't get lost. But if you do say who you are and someone will see you safely home.'

The countryside round the village was quiet, despite the fact that Amsterdam was only a few miles away, and, warmly wrapped in the new winter coat, she and the dogs walked along the narrow brick roads. They met few people, but those she did, greeted her cheerfully. She came to a canal presently, and walked beside it for some distance. The country was very flat, and she could see the village churches dotted here and there in the landscape. They were further away than they appeared to be, however, and so she turned for home.

The walk had given her an appetite, and she ate lunch and then settled down to read by the fire, with the dogs snoozing at her feet. Presently she snoozed off herself, her rather untidy head lolling on the chair cushions.

Which was how Roele found her, sprawled awkwardly, her shoes kicked off, her mouth slightly open. He sat down opposite her, watching her until she stretched and woke and sat up.

'Oh, goodness, I fell asleep. Have you been here long?' She was scrabbling around for her shoes and tucking odd wisps of hair tidily away. 'I went for a long walk and ate too much lunch. I'll go and tidy myself and tell Kulk to bring the tea.'

'You are very nice as you are, and Kulk will be here in a few minutes. Where did you go? As far as the canal?'

Emma decided on the green jersey two-piece for their visit on Saturday. It was simple, the colour flattered her, and if they stayed for dinner it would pass muster. Wrapped in her new winter coat, she got into the car beside Roele, telling herself that she wasn't at all nervous. He had settled Percy and Prince on the back seat and now turned to look at her.

'Nervous? Don't be. They are longing to meet you and I believe that you will like them. They're elderly, but interested in just about everything. They are enthusiastic gardeners, they love the theatre and concerts and they still travel. You met Wibeke—and I have another sister, married with children, living in Limburg, and a brother. He's a doctor too, not married yet. He's at Leiden.'

Which gave her plenty to think about.

Roele drove down towards Den Haag and turned off to Wassenaar on the coast north of that city. Wassenaar was so close to Den Haag that it might be called a suburb, peopled by the well-to-do. But once past the elegant tree-lined roads and villas there was the old village, and past that a stretch of fairly open country bordering the wide sands stretching out to the North Sea. The doctor turned into a narrow lane with a pleasant rather old-fashioned lot of houses on either side, and at one of these he stopped.

Nice, thought Emma, getting out and taking a look. Homely and solid. As indeed the house was. It was red brick, with shutters at the windows and an iron balcony above a solid front door. And the garden, even in winter, was one to linger in.

Not that she was allowed to linger. Roele took her arm and whisked her through the large stout door which a woman was holding open. He flung an arm around her and kissed her plump cheek. 'Klar...' He said something to make her laugh and turned to Emma.

'Klar looks after my mother and father,' he told her. 'She has been with us for even longer than the Kulks.'

Klar shook hands and beamed, and led the

way through the hall to a door at its end and opened it. The room beyond was large, with a great many windows giving a view of the garden beyond. There were plants arranged in it, as well as comfortable chairs and tables and an old-fashioned stove at one end of it. It was warm, light and old-fashioned. Children, thought Emma, would love it.

She gave a small sigh of relief as the two people in it came to meet them. Roele, thought Emma, in thirty years' time: a nice old gentleman in elderly tweeds, still handsome, his eyes as bright and searching as his son's. And his mother—she had tried to imagine her without much success, and she had come nowhere near the plump little lady with hair in an old-fashioned bun and a pretty face, unashamedly wrinkled. Her eyes were blue and she was wearing a dress of the same colour, not fashionable, but beautifully made.

'Mother, Father,' said the doctor, 'here is my wife, Emma.'

She had not known such warmth since her father died. She was welcomed as though they had known and loved her all their lives. She swallowed back unexpected tears and was kissed and hugged and made to sit down beside Mevrouw van Dyke, and over coffee and sugary biscuits she listened to her mother-in-law's gentle kind voice.

'You poor child, you have had little happiness for the last year or so, but now Roele will make you happy again. We are so delighted to have you for another daughter. He has taken a long time to find a wife to love and to be loved by her.'

Presently Emma found herself sitting with the old gentleman. 'Roele has told us so much about you; we feel we know you well already. We don't see as much of him as we should like, for he is a busy man. You will know that already. But you must come and see us as often as you wish. Do you drive? Then he will get you a car so that you can be independent of him.'

Emma murmured agreement, not sure that she wanted to be independent. Roele's company wasn't only a pleasure, she had a feeling that she didn't wish to do without it. Surely he didn't want her to be one of those women who had so many interests outside the home that they were hardly ever there?

She caught his eye across the room and had the feeling that he knew just what she was thinking. That made her blush, and that in turn made Mevrouw van Dyke smile.

Lunch was a light-hearted meal, with cheerful

talk about the wedding, and afterwards Emma
walked round the garden with her father-in-law.
Since she was quite knowledgeable about
plants, flowers and shrubs, they got on fa-
mously.

Later, he told his wife that Roele had married
a splendid girl. 'She knows the Latin names of
almost everything in the garden but doesn't
boast about it. He's met his match!'

His wife knew just what he meant. She said
comfortably, 'Yes, dear. He's met his love too.'

It was late when Roele and Emma got home,
for they had stayed for dinner and sat talking
long after the meal was finished. The house was
quiet, for the Kulks had gone to bed, and they
went into the kitchen to sit at the table drinking
the hot chocolate Katje had left on the Aga, not
saying much, sitting in companionable silence.
Prince and Percy, curled up together in Prince's
basket had given them a sleepy greeting and
dozed off again, and Emma yawned.

'A lovely day,' she said, sleepily content—
only to have that content shattered a moment
later when Roele told her that he was going to
Rome in the morning.

Emma swallowed the yawn. 'Rome?
Whatever for? For how long?'

In her sudden dismay she didn't see the
gleam in the doctor's eyes. There had been

more than surprise on her face; his Emma was going to miss him...

'I have been asked to examine a patient who lives there. I shall be gone for four or five days, perhaps longer. It depends upon her condition.'

'A woman?' said Emma, and he hid a smile.

'Yes, a famous one too. In the entertainment world.'

'How interesting,' said Emma tartly, and got to her feet. 'Shall I see you tomorrow before you go?'

'I'll leave here tomorrow about nine o'clock. Shall we have breakfast about eight?'

She nodded. 'I'll leave a note for Katje.' She went to the door and he went with her and opened it, bending to kiss her cheek as she went past him.

'Goodnight, Emma, sleep well.'

Well, I shan't, thought Emma crossly, intent on lying awake and feeling sorry for herself. Leaving her alone in a strange country while he jaunted off to Italy. And who was this patient? Some glamorous film star, bewitchingly beautiful, no doubt, lying back on lacy pillows in her bed, wearing a see-through nightie...

Emma allowed her imagination full rein and cried herself to sleep.

She went down to breakfast feeling quite contrary, wearing a tweed skirt and a cashmere jumper, wishing to look as much unlike the hussy in the nightie as possible. She had dabbed powder on her nose but forgotten her lipstick, and swept her colourful hair onto the top of her head in an untidy bunch.

The doctor thought she looked adorable, but from the look on her face he judged it hardly the time to tell her so. He enquired instead as to whether she had slept well, passed the toast rack and told her that he would phone her that evening.

'What time will you arrive in Rome?'

'Early afternoon.'

'Then you can phone me when you get there.' That sounded like a suspicious wife, so she added hastily, 'That is, if you have the time.'

'I'll ring from the airport.'

The matter settled to her satisfaction, Emma finished her breakfast, remarking upon the weather, the garden, the dogs—anything but his trip to Rome.

When he had gone, with Kulk beside him so that he could drive the Rolls back from Schipol, she took the dogs for a walk. She was beginning to find her way around now. The countryside wasn't dramatic but it was restful, and there was little traffic. She walked a long way, meeting no one and feeling lonely.

Roele phoned after lunch. His voice reassured

her that the flight had been uneventful and he was about to be driven into Rome.

'I hope you will find your patient not too ill,' said Emma, 'and that you will have some time to enjoy Rome.'

They had had orgies in ancient Rome, she reminded herself. Did they still have them, and would Roele be tempted to go to one? She wasn't exactly sure what one did at an orgy but there would be bound to be beautiful girls there...

Such thinking wouldn't do at all, she told herself. Her imagination was running away with her again. It was only because she liked Roele so much that she wanted him to take care. It was a pity that she couldn't picture him, calm and assured, bending over the bed of a famous singer who had been struck down by some obscure illness which, so far, no one had diagnosed. The bed of the hospital variety, without a lace pillow in sight, and his patient's wan face as white as the all-enveloping garment she was wearing. And, since she was feeling very ill, the doctor could have been an ogre with two heads for all she cared.

There was plenty to keep Emma occupied during the next few days. The *dominee* called to ask her to go with his wife to Amsterdam to buy the small toys to be handed out to the schoolchildren on Sint Nikolaas Eve, and the following day they had to be wrapped in bright paper and stowed away ready for the party. When Roele phoned Emma told him about it, not taking too long, in case he was anxious to ring off. But it seemed he wasn't, for he wanted to know what else she had done, whether the dogs were behaving themselves and had she taken any long walks?

She wanted very much to ask when he was coming home, but surely he would tell her? She was on the point of bidding him a cheerful goodbye when he said, 'I shall be home tomorrow, Emma.'

Before she could stop herself she said, 'Oh, I'm so glad; I've missed you...'

She hung up then, wishing she hadn't said it.

She went to find Kulk and tell him, and discovered that he already knew. He was to take the car to Schipol to pick up the doctor from the plane landing at three o'clock. And would *mevrouw* like to see Katje about dinner for the following day? The doctor was bound to be hungry...

Emma felt hurt. Roele could have told *her* at what time he would arrive, and she could have gone to Schipol to meet him. But he hadn't wanted her.

For the first time since they had married she

wondered if she had made a dreadful mistake. Somehow the close friendship she had felt at Salcombe was dwindling away. Perhaps he was disappointed in her, although she had done her best to be what he wanted. He had said he wanted a friend and a companion, someone who would ease his social life for him and preside at his dinner table when they had guests.

She worried at her thoughts like a dog worrying a bone for the rest of the day, and a good deal of the night. But by the following afternoon she had pulled herself together, deciding she was being silly, imagining things which didn't exist. She put on one of the pretty warm dresses, took pains with her face and subdued her hair into a French pleat. She went downstairs and sat in the drawing room with Prince and Percy and, so as not to look too eager, had a book open on her lap.

She didn't read a word but sat, her ears stretched for the sound of the heavy front door closing, so that the doctor, coming into his house by a side door, caught her unawares.

He stood in the doorway and said, 'Hello, Emma,' in a quiet voice.

She dropped the book and spun round and out of her chair to meet him. She forgot that she was going to be pleased to see him in a cool friendly way; instead she shot across the room and he came to meet her and take her in his arms.

'Well, what a warm welcome,' he said, smiling down at her. He held her a little way from him. 'And how pretty you look. For my benefit, I hope?'

'No, of course not. Well, yes. I mean, you were coming home...' She saw his slow smile and added hastily, 'Was it a success, your visit?'

'I hope so. An obscure chest condition which might bring an end to the lady's singing career.'

He came and sat down opposite her and Kulk brought in the tea tray. Emma felt a very warm contentment.

It was on the following day that he told her that they had been invited to have drinks at the hospital director's house. 'We have known each other some time now, and he has a charming wife. Will you be ready if I get home around six o'clock.'

'Then I'll tell Katje to have dinner ready at eight?'

'Yes, by all means. I should warn you that this is the beginning of an obligatory social round so that you may meet everyone—my colleagues, their wives, old family friends. I did tell you that I knew a number of people.'

'My Dutch...' began Emma.

'No need to worry; they all speak English. I must rely upon you to deal with invitations, and of course we shall have to invite everyone back again.' He smiled at her. 'You can see why I need a wife!'

For some reason his remark depressed her.

CHAPTER NINE

SHE must look her best, decided Emma, getting ready for the drinks party that evening. She brushed her hair to shining smoothness, took pains with her face and got into the dark green velvet dress. Which, even under her critical gaze, was without fault. And Roele's admiring look clinched the matter.

Although she was by no means unused to social occasions, Emma felt nervous. The director of the hospital was an important person, and she wanted to make a good impression and not let Roele down. But she need not have worried. Their host was a middle-aged, scholarly man who appeared to be on the most friendly terms with Roele, and as for his wife, an imposing lady with a rigid hairstyle and ample proportions, she was kindness itself, taking Emma under her wing and introducing her to several other people there.

Going back home later, Emma asked anxiously, 'Was I all right? I wish I could speak

Dutch—your kind of Dutch, not just the odd word.'

'You were a great success, Emma. I have been envied by the men and congratulated by the women and, should you wish, you have a splendid social life ahead of you.'

'Well,' said Emma, 'I like meeting people and going to the theatre and all that sort of thing, but not by myself and not too often. And only if you're there, too.'

'I shall do my best to be on hand, but you will have to go to numerous coffee mornings on your own.'

'I'm going to one in the village tomorrow. A kind of coffee morning the children have got up to raise money for Christmas. All the mothers are going and the *dominee* asked if I would go too. It'll be fun and I can practise my Dutch on the children. I asked Katje to make some biscuits so that I could take something. You don't mind?'

'My dear Emma, of course I don't mind. This is your home in which you may do whatever you like, and I'm glad that you like the village. My mother did a great deal to help the *dominee* and he will be delighted to have your interest.'

The visit to the village was a success; the children accepted Emma's fragmented Dutch in the unsurprised way that children have, and even though she seldom managed to complete a whole articulate sentence no one laughed.

No one laughed at the various coffee mornings she attended either, but then everyone spoke English to her. They were kind to her, these wives of Roele's colleagues, introducing her to an ever-widening circle of acquaintances, concealing their well-bred curiosity about her, making sure that she went to the right shops, dropping hints as to what to wear at the various social functions. Emma took it all in good part, sensing that they wanted to be friends and had no intention of patronising her.

But she didn't allow the social round to swallow her up. She was beginning to understand the running of Roele's house, under Katje's tuition: the ordering of food, the everyday routine, the careful examination of its lovely old furniture, checking for anything that needed expert attention, the checking of the vast linen cupboard. All things which needed to be done without disturbing Roele's busy day.

Besides that, there was the village. She went at least once a week, always with the dogs—to have coffee at the *dominee's* house, to talk to the middle-aged school teacher at the primary school, and join the committee engaged in organising first Sint Nikolaas and then Christmas. Her days were full and she was happy. Though

not perfectly happy, for she saw so little of
Roele.

It sometimes seemed to her that he was
avoiding her. True, they went to a number of
dinner parties, and he once took her to the theatre to see a sombre play in Dutch. She hadn't
enjoyed it, but sitting by him had made her
happy; she saw so little of him...

There was to be a drinks party at the hospital.
'Black tie and those slippery bits and pieces to
eat,' Roele had told her. 'Wear something
pretty. That green thing with the short skirt. It
won't only be hospital staff; there will be the
city dignitaries there as well.' He had smiled at
her. 'Mother and Father will be there, and quite
a few people who know you quite well by now.'

On the evening of the party she went downstairs to the small sitting room and found him
already there, immaculate in black tie, standing
at the open door into the garden where the dogs
were romping.

As she went in he whistled them indoors and
closed the French windows, shutting out the
cold dark evening.

'Charming,' he said, and crossed the room to
her. 'And it's about time we got engaged.'

'But we're already married,' said Emma.

'Ah, yes, but I have always fancied a long
engagement, buying the ring and so on.'

Emma laughed. 'Don't be absurd, Roele. You do all that before you marry!'

'So we must do it after, must we not? I cannot offer to buy you a ring, but perhaps you will wear this one? A family heirloom which gets handed down to each successive bride.'

He had a ring in his hand, a glowing sapphire surrounded by diamonds set in a plain gold band. He slipped it onto her finger above her wedding ring.

'There, they go well together.'

Emma held up her hand to admire it. 'It's very beautiful—and it fits.'

'I remembered the size of your wedding ring and had this one altered.'

He was matter-of-fact, rather like someone who was aware of something which had to be done and did it with as little fuss as possible.

I have no reason to feel unhappy, thought Emma. He had given me a gorgeous ring and I'm a very lucky girl. So she thanked him with just the right amount of pleasure, careful not to gush. Sentiment seemed to have no part in his gift.

The party was a grand and dignified affair, with champagne being offered on silver trays by correctly dressed waiters and sedate women in black dresses and white aprons proffering canapés from wide dishes. It wasn't long before

Emma became separated from Roele and taken under the wing of the director's wife, handed from one guest to the next. They were all kind to her, and the younger men were flatteringly attentive while the younger women bombarded her with questions about the wedding.

She would have liked Roele to be with her but he was at the far end of the large room, deep in conversation with a group of other men, so she did her best to give light-hearted replies without saying much. Roele was a reserved man and wouldn't want the circumstances of their marriage broadcast. She felt a wave of pleasure, remembering his obvious admiration in the drawing room, and earlier, just before they had gone to greet their host and hostess, he had said softly, 'I'm proud of my wife, Emma.'

The evening was half over when she found herself standing beside an older woman, elegantly dressed and discreetly made up. She had a beaky nose and rather small dark eyes. Emma didn't think she liked her, but since she had made some trivial remark it needed to be answered politely.

'So you are Roele's wife. I am surprised that he has married at last, and to an English girl. I wish you both a happy future. You will find everything strange, no doubt.'

'Well, not really,' said Emma, being polite

again but wishing the lady would go away. 'Life here is very much as it is in England, you know.'

'It is perhaps a good thing that he has chosen someone not from his own country. I—we all— thought he was a confirmed bachelor. After all, he was devoted to Veronique. He was a changed man when she went to America. But of course he needs a wife, a domestic background. For a man in his profession that is necessary. I am sure that he has made a very good choice in you.'

The woman was being spiteful and gossipy, thought Emma to herself. She said sweetly, 'I suppose it is natural for people to be curious about our marriage. But everyone I have met so far has been so kind and friendly. I feel quite at home. And I never listen to gossip…'

She was saved from saying more by one of the younger doctors coming to ask her if she would be coming to the hospital ball.

'You must come. Now that Dr van Dyke has you for a partner I don't see how he can make an excuse. He comes and dances once with the director's wife and then goes away again, but now he can dance all night with you. Although he won't get the chance; we shall all want to dance with you!'

'A ball? How lovely. Of course we shall come. When is it to be?'

The beaky-nosed woman said sourly, 'It is an annual event—Roele hasn't done more than put in a token appearance since Veronique went to America.'

'Then we shall have to change that,' said Emma brightly, and was thankful when the young doctor suggested that she might like to go to the buffet with him and have something to eat.

'Mevrouw Weesp is a little—how shall I say?—sour. She is the widow of a former director and now I think she is lonely and not much liked.'

'Poor soul,' said Emma, and forgot her for the moment, for Roele was coming towards her.

'Oh, I'll make myself scarce,' said the young doctor cheerfully.

'Enjoying yourself?' Roele was piling a plate for her with smoked salmon and tiny cheese tartlets. 'You've scored another triumph, Emma.'

'It must be this dress.'

They were joined by some of his friends and their wives and she had no chance to speak to him again.

'A pleasant evening,' observed the doctor later, ushering her into the house and the welcoming flurry of dogs. 'The ball is the next event to which we have to go.'

'That young man I was talking to said you don't stay—only for one dance.' Which reminded her of something.

They had gone to the small sitting room, where Katje had laid out coffee and sandwiches, and she cast down her wrap and kicked off her shoes.

'Someone called Mevrouw Weesp talked to me. Roele, who was Veronique?'

She watched his face become still. 'A girl I once knew. Why do you ask?'

Emma said crossly, 'May I not ask? I'm your wife, aren't I? Husbands and wives don't have secrets from each other.'

'Since you ask, I will tell you. She was—still is—a beautiful woman, and I fell in love with her—oh, ten years ago. She went to America and married there and is now divorced. I met her again last year when I was over there at a seminar.'

'So she wouldn't marry you and you made do with second best. Me.'

'If you think that of me, then perhaps we should discuss the matter when you aren't so uptight.'

'Me? Uptight?' said Emma in a voice which didn't sound quite like her own. 'Of course I'm not. I asked a perfectly civil question about someone you should have told me about ages ago.'

'Why?' he asked slowly. 'It isn't as if you are in love with me, so my past can be of little interest to you. Just as your affair with Derek is of no interest to me.'

Emma exploded. 'Affair with Derek! You know it wasn't an affair... I couldn't bear the sight of him.' She drew a shaky breath, 'But you met her again last year, and she's divorced.'

He was staring at her rather hard. 'Do you mind so much, Emma?'

She was grovelling around for her shoes. 'I don't mind in the least. I'm going to bed.'

In her room she flung her clothes off, got into bed and cried herself to sleep. Even then she didn't realise that she was in love with Roele.

But Roele knew. He knew too that he would have to handle the situation very carefully, and say nothing for a day or so while she realised her feelings for him. He had been patient; he would continue being patient for as long as need be.

Emma went down to breakfast the next morning, half hoping that Roele would have already left the house. But he was there, wishing her good morning in his calm, friendly fashion, passing her the toast, remarking on the mild weather.

'I shall be at the hospital for a good deal of today, but I'll be free to go with you for the St Nikolaas party in the village tomorrow afternoon. Have they got all they want for the children?'

Emma replied suitably, wondering if they were to forget about last night. Well, he might, but I shan't, she reflected, and to make matters worse as he picked up his post, ready to leave, she saw that the top letter bore a USA stamp.

He put a hand on her shoulder as he went, but he didn't give her the light kiss she had come to expect.

She took herself and the dogs for a long walk that morning, and after lunch wrote a long letter to Miss Johnson and a still longer one to Phoebe. After tea Emma went to her room and examined her clothes, finding that it gave her no satisfaction at all; she might just as well wear an old skirt and jumper, for there was no one to see the lovely things she had bought with such pleasure. Wallowing in self-pity, she went downstairs.

Roele was in the small sitting room, stretched out on one of the comfortable armchairs. He was asleep, his tired face relaxed, the lines in it very marked.

Emma, standing there looking at him, knew then.

Her bad temper, uncertainty and bewilderment and self-pity were swept away. She was in love with him—and why hadn't she realised it sooner? She had always loved him, from that first meeting in the bakery shop at Salcombe.

Now they were in a pretty pickle, weren't they? This woman in America, now free to marry him, and he was tied to a wife he had married for all the wrong reasons. She had been feeling sorry for herself when in fact she should be sorry for Roele. He would do nothing about it even if he had given his heart to this other woman, for that was the kind of man he was. So she would have to do something about it. For him to be happy was the one thing which mattered.

He opened his eyes and sat up. 'Hello, I got home earlier than I expected. Have you had a pleasant day?'

'Yes, I took the dogs through the village and along the road by the canal. Would you like tea? Or coffee? Dinner won't be for an hour or so…'

He got to his feet. 'Just time for me to go and see the *dominee* about the Christmas trees…'

So she was alone again, and even if she had

wanted to talk to him he hadn't given her the chance.

They talked over dinner, of course, trivialities which didn't give her an opening to say what she wanted to say, and after the meal he told her that he had work to do and went away to his study. He was still there when she opened the door and wished him goodnight. Perhaps that would have been a good moment, but he was engrossed in a sheaf of papers, and although he got to his feet he had the papers in his hand, obviously waiting to get back to them.

Perhaps tomorrow, thought Emma before she slept.

True, he was home early, and went with her to the village, where she helped distribute plates of food and mugs of lemonade. She was aware that he was having a word with everyone there, listening gravely to the elderlies who had come to have a look, laughing with the younger women, admiring their babies, and then finally handing out the prizes. She could see that he was enjoying himself among people that he had known for most of his life, and that they accepted him as one of themselves. Just as they accepted her, she discovered with pleasure and surprise.

There was an hour or more before dinner when they got home. Emma went into the small sitting room and Roele followed her. He shut the door and said quietly, 'I think that we might have a talk, Emma...'

'Yes, but before you start, did you know that Veronique was free to marry again when you married me?'

The doctor hadn't expected that. He answered quietly, 'No, Emma.'

Emma sat down and Percy climbed onto her lap. 'You see,' she observed, 'that is important...'

He said, suddenly harsh, 'It is not of the slightest importance—' The phone stopped him. He picked it up, said savagely, 'Van Dyke,' and listened. 'I'll take the car to Schipol—give me an hour,' he said finally.

He put the phone down. 'I'm going to Vienna. I'm not sure how long I'll be away.' He was halfway to the door. 'Get Kulk to pack a bag, will you?'

He went into his study and shut the door and she went to find Kulk and ask Katje to have sandwiches and coffee ready.

Fifteen minutes later he had gone.

The next day she was to go to a coffee morning one of the doctor's wives was giving. Since it was being held for charity, she knew that she would have to go.

There were familiar faces there, and several of them knew that Roele had gone to Vienna.

'An emergency,' one of the older women told her. 'All a bit hush-hush—a political VIP shot in the chest, and of course Roele's splendid with chests.' She smiled kindly at Emma. 'But you know that already. You've not heard from him yet?'

'No, he left in a tremendous hurry. He'll ring just as soon as he can spare a minute.'

Her companion laid a kindly hand on her arm. 'I know just how anxious you feel, my dear. Even now, after years of being married to a medical man, I still fuss privately if he goes off somewhere. We are all fond of Roele, we older wives. He is still so young, and brilliantly good at his job. We were so relieved when that woman Veronique—you know about her, of course?' Emma nodded. 'When she went off to America. A most beautiful woman, but with a cold, calculating heart, greedy and selfish.'

Emma said lightly, 'Roele tells me that she is divorced now...'

'Well, thank heaven that he found you. We all think that you are exactly the right wife for him.'

She was, she knew now that she was, but did he know it? She had fitted in very nicely to his life but there was more to it than that...

She was to meet Kulk with the car at the consulting rooms, and she made her way there, passing Juffrouw Smit's house on the way. On impulse, she rang the old-fashioned bell. Juffrouw Smit opened the door, her severe expression softening to a smile.

'Emma, come in. I don't need to go to the consulting rooms until two o'clock and I've just made coffee. You'll have a cup?'

It was more of a command than a query. Emma, awash with coffee already, meekly said that she would love that.

They sat each side of the old-fashioned stove and talked. One didn't gossip with Juffrouw Smit; the weather was discussed, the government torn to shreds, the high price of everything in the shops condemned, and all in a very refined manner, until at last, these subjects exhausted, Emma said, 'May I ask you something, Juffrouw Smit? In the last day or so I have twice been told about someone called Veronique—someone the doctor knew some years ago. I have no wish to pry into his past life, and I know that he would tell me about her, but each time he is about to do so he has to go away in a hurry. If I knew a little more about her it would be easier for me when people talk to me about her.' She looked hopefully at her companion's severe face. 'You do see that, don't you? And you would know about her, because Roele regards you as his right hand.'

Juffrouw Smit's face remained severe, and Emma said in a rather sad voice, 'I dare say you don't wish to talk about it, and I quite understand. I know it isn't important, but I might say the wrong thing. Everyone takes it for granted that I know about her...'

Juffrouw Smit sniffed delicately. 'There is always gossip, and you have probably got the wrong impression from it. I do not feel that it is any business of mine to discuss it with you, Emma. All I will say is that this woman went to America a long time ago and that if the doctor sees fit to tell you about her then he will do so. There is always gossip at these social gatherings, some of it quite unfounded.'

Emma swallowed disappointment. 'I'm sure you're right,' she agreed politely. 'I don't really enjoy coffee mornings and tea parties, but Roele told me to meet as many people as I could so that I would feel at home quickly.' She glanced at her watch. 'I must go. Kulk will be waiting for me. I do hope that I haven't hindered you.'

'No. I'm always glad to see you, Emma. I hope the doctor will be back home soon. You will be going to Wassenaar for Christmas?'

'Yes. All the family will be there. And you? You spend it with family, too?'

'My brother in Utrecht, just for two days, but I shall go again for the New Year.'

At the door she put a hand on Emma's arm. 'You mustn't worry,' she said.

Which was a useless bit of advice, for there was another letter with an American stamp on top of the pile waiting for Roele's return, and, as if that wasn't enough, that evening there was a phone call. It had gone to the consulting rooms and the porter had switched it through to the house, as he always did.

When Emma answered his ring he said gruffly, 'A call from Washington, *mevrouw*. I'm putting it through for you.'

She had understood most of what he had said, but the woman's voice in her ear took her by surprise.

As she was speaking in Dutch, Emma waited until there was a pause in the rather shrill voice.

'I'm sorry, Dr van Dyke is away and I don't speak Dutch. Will you leave a message? He will be back in a few days.'

The voice sounded annoyed, snapping, 'No message.' Then the caller replaced the receiver.

Perhaps whoever it was would ring again, thought Emma. When the porter went off duty he would switch the answering machine on and Juffrouw Smit would check it in the morning as she always did.

Emma got her coat and went into the garden with the dogs. Two letters from America and a phone call within days? They had to be more than coincidence, and surely whoever it was could have at least given their name or a message?

Emma, usually so matter-of-fact and sensible, allowed her imagination to run riot. If only Roele would phone...

He did, just as she had finished dinner. He sounded just as he always did, friendly, unhurried. How was she? What had she done with her day?

She told him, then added, 'There is another letter for you from America, and this evening a—woman—phoned from Washington. She spoke Dutch. She didn't give a name and she wouldn't leave a message.'

He sounded unconcerned. 'Oh, yes. I was expecting a call. I'll get on to Smitty about it. I can't get away for several days, Emma. I hope that when I do get home we shall have a chance to talk. I'm not prepared to go on as we are.'

'Me too. Goodnight, Roele.'

Emma knew what she was going to do. She went and sat down at the little walnut Davenport in the sitting room and began to write a letter. The first attempt was no good, nor was the second, while the third was brief, almost businesslike.

She was going back to Salcombe, she wrote in her rather large writing. She quite realised that their marriage had been a mistake which could luckily be put right. It would have been nice if he had told her himself about Veronique, but luckily she had been told by several people. She quite understood that now Veronique was free he could be happy with his real love.

It would be quite easy, wrote Emma, writing fast and untidily. She would tell everyone that she had to go back and settle some family business and when she had been away for a week or two he could explain.

She didn't pause to consider if he might object to doing this, but signed herself, 'Your friend Emma', before putting the letter in an envelope and into a pocket. She would leave it on his desk in the study when she went.

She sat for a while at the little desk, doodling on the blotting paper, writing his name in various ways, drawing a heart with an arrow piercing it and then adding 'I love you' several times.

'I'm a fool,' said Emma to Percy and Prince, who were watching her anxiously, and she tucked the blotting paper behind the fresh sheets on the pad.

The letter written, she went to her room and packed a small case and her overnight bag. She counted her money and found her passport, then went back to the small sitting room and lifted the phone.

It was too late for a flight, but the overnight ferry from the Hoek didn't leave until midnight. If Kulk drove her in the Rolls she had ample time to get there. There was a helpful girl on the telephone enquiry line, who put her through to the ferry offices, and there was no trouble booking a berth.

Next she went in search of Kulk. She told him she had had an urgent message from England and must get there as soon as possible. 'I've booked on the Hoek ferry. If you'll drop me there, Kulk, I can be ready in less than half an hour.'

'The doctor, *mevrouw*—can you let him know?'

Emma, embarked on her impetuous plan, allowed the lies to flow easily from her ready tongue. 'I couldn't get him, Kulk. He wasn't at any of the places I enquired at. I left a message and I'll phone as soon as I reach England.'

She felt quite sick at the muddle she was weaving, but to get away as quickly as possible was paramount. She had no plan other than that.

The future, for the moment, meant nothing to her.

A worried Kulk drove her to the Hoek, saw her safely on board and turned for home, feeling uneasy.

At one o'clock in the morning the ferry was making heavy work of the rough weather, and Emma, longing for sleep, was seasick.

And at one o'clock in the morning the doctor got back home, ruthlessly cutting short the various social occasions and meetings laid on for him now that his patient was on the way to recovery. He hadn't liked the sound of Emma's voice on the phone, and his patience was exhausted. He would shake her until her teeth rattled, and then kiss her...

He frowned as he put his key in the lock of the small side door which he used if he was called out at night. There was a light on in the passage leading to the kitchen, and as he went in Kulk came to meet him.

'*Mijnheer*, you are back. Thank heaven...'

'*Mevrouw?* She's ill? There's been an accident?'

'No, no.' Kulk explained, then added, 'It didn't seem right that she should go off like that at a moment's notice. But she insisted. I've only been back half an hour or so.'

They were in the kitchen and Roele sat down at the table.

'Sit down and tell me exactly what happened,' he begged calmly.

Kulk put a cup of coffee before him. 'Upset, she was. Said she couldn't get you on the phone and in such a hurry to be away.'

The doctor drank his coffee. He said with outward calm, 'I dare say there is a letter...'

He went along to the sitting room and saw the envelope propped up on the Davenport. He sat down to read it. When he had finished he was smiling. This was a tangle easily untangled...

His eye lighted on the screwed-up papers in the wastepaper basket and he smoothed them out and read them too. Emma had written in a good deal of agitation but her meaning was clear. He saw the pristine blotting paper too, and thoughtfully turned it over.

He was a tired man, but his wide smile erased the lines etched on his handsome face.

Kulk came presently, with more coffee and sandwiches.

'Go to bed, Kulk. I shall need you in the morning.'

He drank his coffee, ate the sandwiches, and went to bed himself, to sleep for the last few hours of the night, knowing exactly what he would do.

He was up early, but Kulk was waiting, offering breakfast.

'I am going over to England this morning. I've arranged for a plane from Schipol and I'll fly to Plymouth. This is what I want you to do. Take the car over tomorrow morning and drive to Salcombe. Let me know when you get there. I shall be at the end cottage on the Victoria Quay. Take an early ferry and get to Salcombe by early afternoon if you can. I'll drive back in time to get the late-evening ferry. I shall have *mevrouw* with me and you can catch up on your sleep in the back of the car.'

Kulk listened gravely. 'Very well, *Mijnheer*. You will need an overnight bag?'

In the kitchen he confided in Katje that whatever it was that had gone wrong was being put right without loss of time.

'And a good thing, too,' said Katje. 'Such a nice young lady she is.'

Emma, her feet once more on dry land, couldn't wait to get to the cottage. It would be quiet there and she would be able to think clearly. It had been borne in upon her that she had acted hastily, and perhaps unwisely, but it was too late to have regrets as she began the tedious journey to Salcombe: first to London, on a train which had no refreshment car, let alone coffee or tea, queuing for a taxi to cross London, then finding that she would have to wait for an hour for a fast train to Totnes.

She had a meal, made up her face, bought magazines which she didn't read and finally got into the train. It left late and stopped every now and then in the middle of nowhere for no apparent reason, so that by the time she reached Exeter and found the train to Totnes she was hard put to it not to scream. But at last she was in Totnes, and getting into a taxi to take her the last twenty miles or so to Salcombe.

It was early evening now, and all she could think of was a large pot of tea and the chance to take off her shoes.

The taxi dropped her off by the pub and she walked the last short distance along the quay to the cottage. She had the key ready in her hand and unlocked the door with a rush of relief, to be taken aback for the moment by the pleasant warmth of the little room. She switched on the light and caught her breath.

Lounging comfortably in one of the armchairs was Roele.

He got to his feet as she stood staring at him. 'There you are, my dear. You must have had a very tiresome journey.'

Emma burst into tears and he took her in his

arms and held her close. 'You shouldn't be here,' sobbed Emma. 'I've left you. Don't you understand?'

'One thing at a time,' said the doctor calmly. 'I'm here because I love you and you're here because you love me. Isn't that right?'

Emma gave a watery snort. 'But you don't love me. There's this Veronique…'

He sighed. 'Ten years ago I believed that I loved her; then she went to America and I haven't given her a thought since.'

'You met her last year.'

'At a friend's house—and I hardly remembered her. Just as you don't remember Derek.'

'She rang up…'

'No, she didn't. That was the secretary of someone I know in Washington who wants me to do a series of lectures.'

Emma mopped her face on the handkerchief he offered her. 'Do you really love me?'

He looked down at her tired tearstained face. 'Yes, my darling, I really love you. I fell in love with you at the bakery and from that moment you have taken over my life.'

'Have I? Have I really? Do you know I didn't know that I loved you, even though I know now that it was when I first saw you? You bought a pasty.'

'My darling girl... And that reminds me. There are pasties for our supper.'

'I'm hungry. Can one be so in love and be hungry too?'

'Undoubtedly.' He smiled down at her as he unbuttoned her coat and pulled off her gloves. 'There's a bottle of champagne too.'

Later, replete with pasty, pleasantly muzzy with champagne, Emma asked, 'How do we get home?'

'Kulk is bringing the car; we will drive home tomorrow.'

'Back home,' said Emma, in a voice so full of content that he felt compelled to sweep her into his arms once more.

She peered into his face—such a handsome face, tired now, so that he looked older than he was, but happy...

'I am so very happy,' said Emma, and she kissed him.

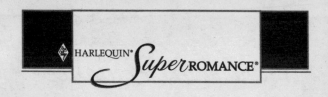

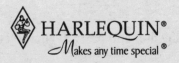

Harlequin®
Historical

From rugged lawmen and
valiant knights to defiant heiresses
and spirited frontierswomen,
Harlequin Historicals will
capture your imagination with
their dramatic scope, passion
and adventure.

Harlequin Historicals...
they're too good to miss!

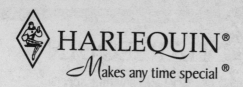

HARLEQUIN®
Makes any time special ®

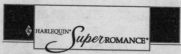

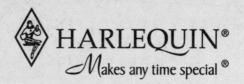
HARLEQUIN®
Makes any time special®

HARLEQUIN®
AMERICAN *Romance*   Upbeat,
All-American Romances

HARLEQUIN®
Duets™   Romantic Comedy

Harlequin®
Historical   Historical,
Romantic Adventure

HARLEQUIN®
INTRIGUE   Romantic Suspense

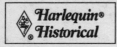
Harlequin Romance®   Capturing the World
You Dream Of

HARLEQUIN® *Presents*   Seduction and passion
guaranteed

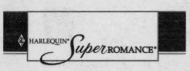
HARLEQUIN® *Super*ROMANCE®   Emotional,
Exciting, Unexpected

HARLEQUIN®
Temptation   Sassy, Sexy, Seductive!

Visit us at www.eHarlequin.com   HDIR2